This story is set in a li... Court in the town of ... England. The street is ... pandemonium, the pe... earth, wonderful characters who live there, and their outrageously naughty doings. Casey's Court is a little corner of the past, where life has remained unchanged for so long that it's almost as though it's been caught in a time-warp. For every one of the raw, no-nonsense folk down Casey's Court, there must be hundreds of you who can recognize them and identify with them. Because you'll still find one or another down your street, if you look hard enough.

JO FOX

Casey's Court

GRAFTON BOOKS

A Division of the Collins Publishing Group

LONDON GLASGOW
TORONTO SYDNEY AUCKLAND

Grafton Books
A Division of the Collins Publishing Group
8 Grafton Street, London W1X 3LA

A Grafton Paperback Original 1989

ISBN 0-586-20561-6

Printed and bound in Great Britain by
Collins, Glasgow

Set in Times

Monday, July 20th, 1987 (Milton Keynes, in the south of England)

What a shock to discover that my 'upright and respectable' husband, Vernon Jolly, was nothing but a liar, a cheat and a womanizer. He used to say, 'When I go, I hope it's while I'm making whoopee!' Well, he got his wish. I wouldn't have minded, but it wasn't me he was making whoopee with when he went. It was a fat peroxide blonde, who took great delight in telling the whole world about it.

Oh, the shame! If I've read the newspaper article once, I've read it a dozen times – her every word emblazoned on my mind. 'It was dreadful!' she told the coroner at the inquest. 'There we were, making wild passionate love one minute. And the next, he gave out two great rattling sighs – one from each end, your honour – then, grabbing me hard in a soft spot,' (she gave a revolting little giggle here and swept her dolly blue eyes over everyone to make sure they were listening) 'well, he sort of shuddered and collapsed in a heap on top of me. I ask you. What else could I do but scream and scream? It wasn't my fault the neighbours thought I was being attacked when they rushed in and threw him out of the window!'

After she'd had a little cry, she told one and all what a 'frightening experience' it had been. Serves her right! It might teach her to keep her grubby little mitts off married men. And if she hadn't swiftly departed from the area, I might have treated her to another 'frightening experience'.

As it is, she's footloose and fancy-free, while I'm well and truly lumbered. Oh, what a pile of troubles Vernon Jolly left me! Two thoroughly spoiled children from his first marriage, a list of creditors a mile long, and a house being sold over my head to pay off the wolves baying at the door. I can't hold up my head when walking down the street. And whoever thought the day would come when I'm actually hiding from the Avon lady? (I owe her £1.20 for wrinkle-removing cream which didn't work on account of the leathery texture of my skin.)

I've had enough shocks to turn a chimney-sweep white overnight. On top of which, there's a most ominous, official-looking letter which I daren't open. It's addressed to me – Mrs Jessica Jolly – and it's marked URGENT in bold red letters. I've propped it up on the dresser where I can see it. It's making me very nervous, but I'll have to summon up the courage to open it soon. I suspect it's notice to quit the house. Either that, or it's the undertaker demanding his money. (Dear God, if you're listening, you might consider helping this one of your flock, seeing as the only other favour I've ever asked of you was over twenty years ago, when I fell in love with Arthur Askwith. And you didn't do that right, did you? Because, as it turned out, he was only after my stamp collection.)

Tuesday, July 21st

I was wrong about that letter being notice to quit the house. That came this morning from the building society. It sneaked up on me in a bright blue harmless-looking envelope, together with four others – one threatening to disconnect the electricity, and another saying that 'unless payment was forthcoming' they would turn off the gas. The third was demanding payment on the furniture. And the last one was from the insurance people, saying I was wrong to assume there was any money owing to me, because Vernon Jolly had not paid any premiums for some considerable time and all policies had lapsed long ago.

Dear God, this is my second prayer in less than twenty-four hours, so you must see how desperate I am. Please make a miracle happen? Not a big one. Just enough to provide a roof for this family, with the occasional meal thrown in. And God, I understand it's hard for little Tom to accept that his dad's gone. But will you please stop him from doing unspeakable things in his new trousers? I know he's only four, and I should make allowances, but I really am beside myself! Three times today he's tied the dustbin to Lucky's tail. The poor dog went berserk. He ran amok right through my best pansies, ending up lodged between two conifers and wailing as if the bats of hell were on his tail. The two ginger toms from next door scampered up the tree and watched with great amusement – I swear they were grinning from ear to ear.

Wednesday, July 22nd

Now I've got two of those official-looking letters. They're standing side by side on the dresser and making me doubly nervous.

The telephone's been cut off. The newsagent came banging on the door. 'I'm sorry, Mrs Jolly,' he said, with a most pitiful look, 'I feel for you – I really do! But unless the paper bill's paid today I have to cancel your order.' I haven't any money, so I won't get any more papers. He's just one more added to the long list of creditors. (Thank you, Vernon Jolly.)

Thursday, July 23rd

When I looked in the mirror this morning I couldn't believe my eyes. Jessica Jolly, I said to that thin red-haired person with bags under her brown eyes and a face so haggard I could hardly credit it was the same thirty-five-year-old woman who, only a few short weeks ago, was happily kicking up her legs with the rest of those admirable keep-fit fanatics with nothing much better to do, Jessica Jolly, I said, you'd better pull yourself together, my girl.

I reminded myself about seven-year-old Wilhelmina, four-year-old Tom, a five-bedroomed house and contents which were no longer mine, and an eight-year-old love-able black and white mongrel with short legs and long floppy ears. Think about them, I told myself – they're your responsibility now. It was a foolish thing to do. Now I feel ten times worse. I can see only one solution, and that's to run away and leave them all.

If only I had a relative I could talk to – but there isn't one. My own parents died a while back and I'm an only child. According to what Vernon Jolly told me in the four years we were married, his father was dead, his mother, Maggie, had disappeared, and his brother (aged forty-two, some two years older than Vernon) was a bit of a wanderer and they'd lost touch.

So, his first wife having married an American and gone over there to live, there was no one at all to whom I could turn. The DHSS can't help, so they say – not until the house is sold. And, if there's anything left from that, they reckon they won't be able to help at all. (I'll be lucky if there's enough left to buy a horse and cart – though it might just come to that.)

The clerk I saw suggested I should think about having

Lucky put down – 'It will help ease the burden a little,' she said, with a terrifying smile. I suppose I was fortunate not to have seen an even more heartless clerk – one who might have suggested I put the children and myself down as well.

Friday, July 24th

I don't feel at all well. It was terrible getting Wilhelmina to go to school. The trouble started when I had to share the remaining cornflakes between her and Tom. She ended up with nine – but swears Tom had two extra. There was such a fight! She and Tom were going at it hammer and tongs when I came into the kitchen. I rushed in to separate them, and Lucky thought I was playing, dived between my legs and sent me head first into the sideboard. The jolt knocked down a big brass horse, which smacked Lucky right between the eyes and put him out for the count.

Lucky's got a black eye and a huge lump on the top of his head. I've got a blinding headache, and the children have got sore posteriors where I heartily smacked them. And I don't care if they're not speaking to me. But I do wish Tom hadn't taken his revenge by doing unmentionable things in his trousers. (My nerves are going!)

Saturday, July 25th

What a day! Lucky's been staggering about like a drunk. Tom and Wilhelmina are still giving me the silent treatment, and those two letters have been staring at me all the time. The hoover's packed up, my best pansies have

9

wilted, and the meat I got at a bargain price smells to high heaven.

Tiffany from next door came to the rescue with a pound of sausage meat, which she said was left over from the pâté she'd been making. (That was a little fib, because I know for a fact that it's her poodle's weekly treat.) She's not a bad sort. Funny, though, how your 'friends' desert you in times of trouble. Tiffany's the only one still speaking to me, and even she creeps in the back way, frightened the neighbours might see her. 'Don't forget,' she protested, when I mentioned it to her, 'when you've gone, I still have to live here.' Let's hope her darling husband doesn't do a Vernon Jolly on her – he's given me the glad eye more than once! And I've come to the conclusion that no woman ever really knows what her man's getting into. (More often than not, it's a fat peroxide blonde!)

Sunday, July 26th

Lots of questions today from the children – they wanted to know why we hadn't got any money and what was going to happen to us when everything was sold by 'the nasty men'. I explained as gently as I could that they were not to worry, because I'd think of something. What upset them most was my telling them that everything in the house would probably have a number stuck on it and be sold off. 'What! My bath-duck as well!' Tom demanded, his big brown eyes trembling with tears. The only way I could pacify them both was to take them round to Willen Lake to see the ducks. That was a mistake. Lucky chased the ducks, the children chased Lucky, and a huge gander chased the lot of them. I thought it was going to bite Tom on his rear end, but for some reason it veered off at the last moment to hide itself in the bushes, every now and then poking out its head, hissing, and daring anybody to come near it.

I took the two letters out with me. I really did intend to open them, but chickened out. At five o'clock we'd eaten all the jam sandwiches and were ready to go back. At last the children were talking to me again – until Wilhelmina started wailing about there soon being 'no home to go back to'. Tom sobbed that he didn't want his bath-duck to 'have a number stuck across his beak'. And how could he finish his lego-garage when 'the nasty man wants to take it away'?

I must admit, I didn't help matters when I said that if they didn't both behave themselves I'd let the nasty man take them away as well. Now they've both gone silent again. I really don't think I was cut out to be a mother.

After they were washed and in bed, I sat in the chair, playing about with all sorts of ideas. Would we end up in one of those bed and breakfast hostels the DHSS put you in when you've nowhere to go? Could I perhaps get a live-in job somewhere – after all, I was quite a good cook? Or would there be enough money left for us to get a caravan? All kinds of notions went through my mind. Then, out of the corner of my eye, I caught sight of a small trim figure with fair hair and grey nervous eyes creeping in by the back door. It was Tiffany. 'I've been clearing out my cupboards,' she said apologetically, 'and I thought you might find a use for these.' She dumped two loaves, a carton of eggs and a block of butter on the table, for which I thanked her.

'I'm sure Lucky will enjoy them,' I said, thinking: *Thank the Lord we'll have a bit of breakfast tomorrow after all*.

All the same, her kindness prompted me to confide in

her about those two letters – I had to talk to somebody about them, before they drove me mad. When she offered to open them I jumped at the chance, coward that I am. And now I'm as intrigued as ever, because they were both from a solicitor who was 'extremely anxious' that I should contact him at the earliest opportunity. The second was more pressing than the first.

'He says he may be able to show you something to your advantage,' Tiffany exclaimed, growing excited. I remained cautious, though – if only because Vernon Jolly had said the very same words to me on the night we met at the Palais. And look what I got then!

Still, it wasn't bad news, was it? But how good it might be remains to be seen. I shall contact this Mr Darling first thing tomorrow. (I hope it's that little miracle I asked God for.)

Monday, July 27th

I love Mr Darling! After we'd walked Wilhelmina to school this morning, I phoned the firm of Darling and Darling to say I was on my way. Tom cried the whole time in the telephone-box. It was a pity he saw me raiding his piggy-bank for a couple of ten pence coins.

At ten o'clock we were seated in the solicitor's office – Tom and I on one side of an enormous highly polished desk, and the bald, bespectacled Mr Darling on the other. He had the most unnerving habit of stretching his neck and looking down his nose while he was talking, so that I found myself counting the stubby hairs on his chin and watching mesmerized as his protruding adam's apple bobbed up and down with every word.

When he told me that I had been left a property by a

12

dim and distant relative, I had to restrain myself from leaping out of the chair to hug him. It was only later that I was to learn just how dim had been the relative and how distant was the property. The added information that it was originally a business, but had been closed for some time, triggered off some grand ideas. Me – Jessica Jolly – the sole owner of a business, no less! There you are, I told myself, it just goes to show. You can be flat broke one minute, with no prospects whatsoever, and the next you're a property-owner and businesswoman.

Bit by bit I was brought down to earth, until I was disappointed, then astonished, and finally totally horrified. 'Up north!' I shrieked (with a gusto which set little Tom crying – after which there crept into the air a most unpleasant and persistent smell).

'That's right, Mrs Jolly,' Mr Darling confirmed, rising from the comfort of his padded leather chair to throw open the window behind him. Before coming back to the subject in hand, he gave me a most suspicious and disapproving look. 'I'm sorry. I didn't realize the news would be such a shock to you.' It dawned on me. He thought it was *I* who had contaminated the air with the undesirable aroma! And for a portly gentleman, he moved surprisingly quickly. He thrust the entire batch of documents across the desk, opened the office door and nipped smartly out into the corridor, saying, 'Look over those papers, sign them and post them back to me as soon as possible. Upon their receipt, I will forward you the keys and relevant papers. Good luck to you, Mrs Jolly.'

When Tiffany came round this evening, I'd read right through the papers and had decided what to do. She didn't agree.

'But it would be better to sell it, wouldn't it, Jessica?' she pointed out. 'Then, with the money, you could rescue this house and pay off all the bills.'

'That was my first thought, too,' I told her, and so it had been – until I saw that the 'property' was an old run-down barber's shop in a terrace of back-to-back houses, tucked away in the oldest part of a northern industrial town. 'It says here that I'd be lucky to get eight thousand for it.'

'Eight thousand!' Like me, she was flabbergasted. 'There must be some mistake, Jessica. A place like that, even in terrible condition, would cost sixty thousand round here.'

'Yes. Round here. But we're talking about the old industrial north. A place called Casey's Court, in Oswaldtwistle.'

'What? You mean like . . . sort of . . . Coronation Street?'

'Exactly! Only it seems the property I've inherited is not quite as smart as that.' I went on to explain how Vernon Jolly had left me with a fifty-thousand-pound mortgage, a pile of debts amounting to somewhere in the region of another fifty thousand, and a house and contents which just might not scrape together enough to pay them off.

'So you see,' I told her, 'I've no choice but to move up there and make the best of it.'

Her response was to stare into space, murmuring over and over, 'Oh dear, I had no idea it was as bad as that.'

Whereupon Wilhelmina and Tom dashed in from their hidey-hole where they'd been eavesdropping, one crying 'I don't want to live in Coronation Street, I don't like Percy Sugden', and the other clutching his bath-duck and pleading 'You won't let the nasty man stick a number on *me*, will you?' I took one look at Wilhelmina's tearful hazel eyes and her long brown hair all tousled about her little shoulders, then at the boy's big dark eyes and pouting mouth, his little chubby arms clutching that yellow duck, and in a minute we were all crying our eyes out and clinging to each other as if it was the last day of the world. When Tom made his own special protest Tiffany fled, saying she'd be back. I expect she'll pop in to see us before we go.

I wonder if this inheritance will prove to be another millstone round my neck, or a blessing in disguise? It's a certainty I can't afford the repairs that obviously need doing. Still, at least it's a roof over our heads, and there's no mortgage to pay. When I'd put the children back to bed I remembered Coronation Street with renewed interest. It's all right *watching* all those strange goings-on, but how could we ever fit in up north? We'll have to say 'Iyer, cock – ecki thump' and eat hot-pot. And I do see what Wilhelmina means – I hope there aren't any Percy Sugdens where we're going.

Well, thank you, God. Although you shouldn't have taken me so literally when I said I didn't mind if the miracle was little. And did you have to send me one that was falling apart? If you have any more in mind, could you possibly make them just a *bit* bigger?

I think I'll stop asking for miracles. When I said a bit bigger I didn't mean the size sixteen form of Maggie Flaherty!

There she was at quarter past eight this morning, standing on the doorstep, suitcase in hand and thrusting out a photograph of Vernon Jolly as a baby, nude. When she told me she was my mother-in-law, I nearly fainted. When I told her that her precious son had gone the way of all philanderers, *she* nearly fainted.

When she'd recovered enough to knock back the last of the brandy, I took a good long look at her. She wasn't at all how I'd always thought of her. She was on the tall side, big-boned, with an upright carriage and a severe authoritative way of looking at you through narrowed blue eyes. And she wore one of those patronizing expressions which said, 'But of course you can speak your mind, dear. Yes, I will listen, but don't fool yourself that your opinion will make the slightest impression on me.' I wasn't surprised to find her name was Maggie. 'Flaherty was my fourth husband's name,' she told me with a shake of her head, 'and now I'm all alone in the world.'

I would have pressed her as to where Mr Flaherty was, but she looked about to burst into tears. I assumed he was no longer with us, no doubt keeping Vernon company. 'Oh, I am sorry,' I said, and left it at that.

It turns out that Maggie Flaherty, my newly acquired mother-in-law, has it in mind to park herself on me for the duration. 'Look here,' I told her, in my kindest yet firmest voice, 'I'm up to my neck. There are huge debts to settle and no money, and if it hadn't been for a small inheritance I've just come into we'd all be wandering the streets.' I told her that she would have to find somewhere else to live. 'I'm very sorry, but that's the way of things, Mrs Flaherty.' I made no bones about it. 'I'll make you a cup of tea, then you'll have to be on your way.' I felt heartless, but I was adamant. After all, I don't know her, do I? She claims to be Vernon Jolly's mother, but for all I know she could be old Nick in disguise.

2 A.M., *on waking from a nightmare*

I do hope Maggie's comfortable in the spare bed. She did seem pleased when I called her Mother, and assured her that she was most welcome to move up north with us. We talked well into the night, and if I'd had any doubts about her being my mother-in-law she quickly dispelled them with her intimate revelations concerning Vernon Jolly. One in particular only a lover or a mother could have known about, and by no stretch of the imagination could I see even Vernon Jolly jumping into bed with a sixty-five-year-old tank.

Anyway, Maggie Flaherty talked me round. She'll be living with us from now on, poor soul. I finally decided that I wouldn't have been able to forgive myself if I'd turned out an old woman. Besides, it seems old man Flaherty left her a few thousand pounds. On top of which, she said, 'I've learned a few skills over the years, dear. I'm a dab hand about the house, you know – why, I can turn my hand to almost anything.' Then, eyeing the two children out of the corner of her eye, she whispered, 'I would be obliged, though, if you'd keep *them* away from me. I'm not partial to little people.' I know just how she feels.

Thursday, July 30th

All the arrangements are made. We're moving up north to Casey's Court on Saturday!

Maggie's so organized, it's too good to be true. She's booked one of those small self-drive vans and she will drive us up there, with our few personal possessions – together with a rather large chest which suddenly appeared on our doorstep, addressed to Maggie Flaherty and, according to her, 'full of memories, dear'. Ah, well, we're all entitled to a few of those, are we not?

Friday, July 31st

I took all the papers back to Mr Darling's office and collected the keys to No. 2, Casey's Court. They look like a bunch of stone-age tools. There's a great big rusty one, two round-barrelled ones and a long thin object with a bulbous tip. (I won't repeat what Maggie Flaherty had to say about that one. Suffice to say she suddenly had fond memories of her four husbands.)

Wilhelmina took one look at the keys and started bawling. 'They're going to put us in a dungeon!' she told little Tom, who promptly hid in the outside shed, with his yellow duck under his arm. I believe this whole business could have serious psychological repercussions on those children's later years.

Lucky's digging up every bone he's ever buried, and piling them on the patio. The garden looks like a minefield.

Saturday, August 1st

I'm writing in my diary early today, for two reasons. One, I'm both too excited and too terrified to keep everything bottled up, and two, in the complete and utter chaos which I'm sure must follow our every step this fateful day, I may not remember where I've put the blessed thing.

Maggie's gone to get the van. Lucky's guarding his pile of bones like a dog possessed, Tom won't come out of the bathroom, and Wilhelmina's threatening to throw herself out of the bedroom window. (Like father, like daughter!)

Tiffany's been round with a pile of blankets. 'They might come in useful,' she said, unable to resist adding: 'They're obsolete in our house, since we got our new continental quilts.' She came back a second time with an old set of saucepans and two horrific lampshades. I *am* grateful, but I can't help suspecting she sees it as a heaven-sent opportunity to get rid of all her jumble.

It seems Tiffany's not the only one. I've just looked out of the window. Piled in the middle of the front lawn is so much old furniture, bedding and other articles that for a minute I thought somebody was building a bonfire. I've shovelled the bones off the patio and heaped them up at the front gate. Lucky's guarding them with his fangs bared. That'll keep the vultures away.

I wrapped all my personal knick-knacks up in old newspaper and packed them in a cardboard box. I would have taken a few other things, like the Doulton figurine and the best cutlery set, but 'the nasty man' already has everything of value on his list. The children decided they'd wrap up a few of their bits and pieces. What a fuss! Crying and fighting and breaking things in a tug of war – poor Teddy will never be the same again. I'm afraid I lost my temper when they started scattering the newspaper all over the place. At one point, the pair of them were in stitches over a photograph of a poor woman who – according to Wilhelmina's best reading ability – had escaped from a nearby 'Menthol Institution' and was described by one member of staff as 'a right nutter'.

By this time, I was on the point of wrenching out every hair on my head. So when Tom began jumping up and down and squealing 'Maggie's a nutter! Maggie's a nutter!' I threatened to slap his legs, snatched the paper out of his hands and squashed it between my artefacts. I know the children haven't taken to Maggie Flaherty, but I won't have them using every opportunity to make fun of the poor dear. After all, she's the only one amongst us who has experience of plumbing – and she is paying for the van. She also happens to be their grandmother – even if the thought does sicken her. Being their stepmother sickens *me*. But we all have our crosses to bear.

I've arranged for Tiffany to send the house-keys to the solicitor. So, here we are, all ready and waiting for Maggie to get back with the van. The two monsters are squatting on the step sulking; I've had a last minute look round my beautiful home, and a good cry. All the neighbours are peeping from behind their curtains and Tiffany's sniffling into her exquisitely embroidered handkerchief. Lucky's having a vicious fight with a stray pekingese – meanwhile, behind his back, the neighbourhood dogs are making off with his precious bones.

My God! This can't be Maggie, can it? It *is*! Surely we can't be expected to travel over two hundred miles in that rusting heap? 'What *is* it?' I asked, peering aghast from a safe distance. Lucky had backed away, growling, and the monsters were hiding behind me.

'What is it!' She was evidently put out. 'It's ours, that's what it is. I might tell you that in its day this little car was considered to be a rich man's plaything.' It looked like a poor man's cast-off to me.

Maggie was most upset, explaining in graphic detail how she had decided it made more sense to buy a vehicle than to hire one. 'It's bound to come in handy,' she argued, pointing out, also, that if we didn't need it at the other end we could sell it. I couldn't help but doubt whether we would ever get to the other end. As we stuttered away down the road amidst a cloud of smoke and confusion, I wondered what other surprises the Lord had in store for us.

Sunday, August 2nd

I'm still in shock.

Monday, August 3rd

I should never have considered running away instead of coming to Casey's Court. I should have done it with all speed.

After a six-hour nightmare journey (which should have taken only half that time in a proper vehicle with four round wheels and an engine that didn't refuse to budge more than eight miles without a bucket of water thrust down its throat) we drew – no, not 'drew' – we *staggered* into Oswaldtwistle. Whereupon, obviously thinking it had completed its life's work, the heap of rust shuddered gently and collapsed on to the tarmac. No amount of cajoling, kicking, threatening or abusing could persuade it to carry us the rest of the way. Maggie took control, and within the hour a taxi arrived to pick us up. What a sorry lot we must have looked. There we were on the grass verge, with little Tom fast asleep across my box of artefacts, the tears still wet on his face and such a look of innocence about him that, at that moment anyway, I could have forgiven him anything (well, almost anything). Wilhelmina had climbed up a tree in a fit of sulks, only to find she was stuck and couldn't get down again. It served her right. 'You can bawl all you like,' I told her, 'as far as I'm concerned you can stay there, you sulky little madam!' Maggie obviously felt the same way, because she turned her back on the little horror as well. Even Lucky had an opinion – aptly demonstrated when he scowled up at her, gave out a disapproving yap and peed up the tree-trunk.

The taxi-driver (obviously having no experience of little madams) said, 'Poor little thing,' and helped her down with the utmost care. I couldn't quite hear what he said when she promptly kicked him in the shins.

There was no mistaking his reaction, however, when we were all piled in his taxi and I gave him the address. His eyes spun round in their sockets. 'Tha's gooin' weer?' he exclaimed (whatever that meant), whereupon one and all had something to say. Maggie decided the fellow was double-dutch.

Wilhelmina stared at him. 'What's "weer"?' she demanded.

And little Tom hid his rubber-duck in his trousers. 'It's the nasty man!' he cried, 'and he's *not* having my friend.'

'Did thi say number two, Casey's Court – the old barber's shop as was?' the taxi-driver insisted. When I confirmed it, he said, 'Well, I'm buggered!' (Three times he said that, and each time my heart fell like a stone.)

'Cheer up, Jessica,' Maggie prompted, digging me hard with her elbow. 'It can't be as bad as all that, surely?'

She changed her tune when we'd driven through the town centre and away from the nicer houses. Each time we approached a pleasant-looking area our hopes were raised – then dashed as we sped deeper into the past. We passed derelict cotton mills and acres of wasteland where once had stood row upon row of Victorian back-to-back terraced houses, laid low to make room for new developments.

'It's nobbut a spit away, now,' the taxi-driver assured us, gripping the wheel hard as the car careered off the tarmac road and on to an old cobbled street. In a minute, we were squeezing over the narrowest little bridge I've ever seen. When we came off at the other end, it was as if we'd crossed the time-barrier.

I once saw a film which starred Gary Cooper and a thousand Indians. In one scene Gary Cooper was in charge of a fort in the middle of nowhere, and the Indians were converging on it from all sides. Exactly like the scene before us – only the fort was Casey's Court, and the Indians were armies of bulldozers and little men in flat caps.

Casey's Court was a small cul-de-sac of tiny Victorian back-to-back houses. The front doors opened on to the flagstoned pavement, which was lined with ancient gas-lamps that had been adapted to electricity. Each one depicted a huge red rose of Lancashire, beautifully carved into the jutting arm beneath where the mantle used to be. The street was cobbled and bursting with people – women standing about in busy little groups, men showing off their whippets to each other, children playing hopscotch on the numbers they'd chalked all over the pavement, stray mongrels fighting and chasing each other. And, believe it or not, a horse and cart parked alongside the kerb! 'That's ol' Bill,' offered the taxi-driver. 'Took over that rag-a-bone cart fro' 'is dad, some thirty year back. 'E'll never change, will ol' Bill – 'e's part o' the scenery round these 'ere parts.'

Some two-thirds of the way down on the right-hand side, there protruded from high up the wall the longest orange and white striped pole I have ever seen. It appeared to dominate that whole street, its coloured stripes standing out vivid amongst the greys and browns of houses and cobbles.

'There ye are, lass!' The taxi-driver pointed to the pole. 'That's number two – the ol' barber's shop, as was. By eck! I've lost count o' the number o' times ol' Pops 'as lopped off my 'air! What! Afore 'e was took bad, there were allus a queue a mile long at yon shop. Oh, aye! 'E were a good ol' barber, were ol' Pops!'

The old shop was appalling! The door and window-frames were rotting, two windows were broken, and when we managed to get the front door open there was a pile of mail behind it, ankle deep. 'How long is it since old Pops passed away?' I asked the driver, thinking it must have been some years before.

'Nobbut six month, I should think,' came the answer. 'Ol' Pops never was one to worry about appearances. But the old place does seem to 'ave gone to rack an' ruin, don't it, eh?'

The same could be said of the inside. The front parlour, where old Pops used to cut people's hair, still had the odd curl lying on the floor. There were two grand enough barber's chairs in here, and two handbasins with a few well-stocked wooden shelves above. The back parlour contained two brown high-backed leather chairs set round a big black fire grate, a long darkwood sideboard and a big wooden rocking-chair. The scullery had only a cracked pot-sink, the tiniest gas-cooker, a drop-leaf table and two stiff ladder-back chairs. One wall had shelves from top to bottom, each cluttered with all manner of paraphernalia including some pretty blue cups and plates. The lavatory was outside, across a flagstoned yard, which straight away prompted a volley of protests from Maggie and the monsters. I wasn't too keen, either.

The narrow staircase was hidden in the scullery, behind a door. Upstairs, there were three minute bedrooms (more like cupboards, really). In one were two small brass beds and an orange-box, upended, for a bedside cabinet. There was no wardrobe, but hanging from the picture-rail were two grubby-looking suits. The other two bedrooms each had just a single bed and a stiff little chair with a wicker bottom.

The whole house was buried beneath a two-inch layer of dust. There were no rugs or carpets, only bare floorboards. And the damp musty smell which permeated every room was suffocating (although at least it successfully camouflaged that other aroma which was always with us).

'Looks to me as if the only room old Pops ever bothered about was the barber's shop.' Maggie was quite impressed with the professional way it was laid out. 'I used to do a short back and sides myself, in the days of my youth.' In a strange way, I was glad that Maggie had turned up when she did. I was grateful for her company – especially when we discovered all services had been cut off. 'I'll see about that in the morning!' she promised

Late entry

When the taxi-driver had gone, things looked at their worst as it began to get dark and the two children wouldn't stop crying. It was then that there came a knock on the door. When I opened it, in came an army of people, some in flowered pinnies, some in flat caps. And every one carrying a little gift! Candles, coal for the fire, and even a teapot full of tea! One dear soul had a plate of hot pies, and the wonderful smell set my stomach churning. 'You'll luv 'em, lass,' she said with a broad warm smile. 'They're stuffed full o' taters an' juicy bits o' best mince . . . an' there's a few prime onions chopped in 'em as well.' She set the tray down on the kitchen table with great reverence. 'Them's straight outta t'oven,' she smiled. 'Gerrem down yer while they're still bubblin' 'ot.'

We were all four of us speechless, as, in a matter of minutes, the folk had come and gone, saying little, but nodding and smiling as they went.

I have to admit it – I was close to tears. I've never before experienced anything like what's just happened here. Total strangers, and every one with a heart of gold. 'Oh, Maggie,' I sniffed, 'what kind and wonderful people! I could never imagine such a thing happening down south where we lived.'

'Like as not, you'd be moved in for six months before you exchanged words with a living soul,' Maggie agreed. Then, helping the little ones to tuck into those 'meat an' tater pies', she chuckled, 'I reckon we'll like it here, Jessica.'

My sentiments exactly. Thank you, God. I know I asked for a big miracle, but you've sent an army of little ones instead. They're wonderful! *You're* wonderful. I do believe we'll be all right in Percy Sugden country after all.

Tuesday, August 4th

I'm worn out. Both my hands are covered in blisters, my feet ache and my back feels broken. Maggie makes me feel tired just watching her. I've never seen so much energy in a woman past sixty (nor one past twenty, come to think of it). And there's still a mountain of work and cleaning to do. On top of everything, Lucky's gone missing.

On the plus side, Tom hasn't disgraced himself for a whole twenty-four hours, and Wilhelmina's found a playmate from three doors down. She brought her in earlier – a bright freckle-faced child with hair the colour of carrots and two front teeth missing. "Ow do, Missus Jolly,' she said boldly, which was fine. It was only when she muttered 'I've been moitherin' me mam fer a scen in 'ere' that I remembered we were among foreigners.

Wilhelmina soon put me right, though – well, she would, wouldn't she? 'What Winnie means,' she said scornfully, 'is that she's been worrying her mother to let her have a look at this place.'

'Oh, thank you for the helpful interpretation,' I said. 'And now she's "'ad a scen" you can both get from under my and your grandmother's feet!' Whereupon they scarpered. (Why do I get this awful cringing sensation under my skin whenever there are children about?)

Wednesday, August 5th

I'm surprised there's no word yet from the solicitor. I don't like living off Maggie, though she assures me I'm not to worry. 'You can pay me back at twenty per cent interest,' she said. She wasn't smiling at the time. And

27

she tots up every little expense in her black book. You know, I'm getting a sneaky feeling that she's a member of the Mafia. I was not surprised when she told me that Margaret Thatcher was her hero.

Maggie brought a paper in today. There was an article in it about Jeffrey Archer and the half-million or so he won in that court case. Apparently he's been inundated with begging letters. How disgusting! (Now I know why he still hasn't answered mine.)

Thursday, August 6th

Lucky's still missing. Tom still hasn't lapsed. And Wilhelmina's gone quiet because there's an open day at school for all the new children, and I'm taking her to meet the headmistress tomorrow. 'Winnie's mother lets her stay off school whenever she wants,' she moaned, pouting in her old aggravating fashion.

'Oh, does she?' I retorted. 'Well, *you're* not skiving school – do I make myself clear, young lady?' She didn't answer. Instead, she gave me a sly look and a toss of her head and marched up to her bedroom.

I would have marched after her, but Maggie held me back. 'Let her go,' she said. 'She'll be the first to give in.' Maggie still has a lot to learn about our darling Wilhelmina.

Friday, August 7th

We now have the gas and electricity on, and the telephone reconnected. Maggie Flaherty's an absolute wonder! Oh, I know she seems a bit fanatical at times, the way she rushes about ordering and organizing – but we're all labouring under stress. It was unnerving, though, when she dug out an old World War One tin hat from her chest and rammed it over her ears. When she began marching up and down shouting 'Rally the troops! Rally the troops!' I suddenly found the energy to rush out and scrub the outside lavatory. She followed me and, brandishing the yard-broom over her shoulder, took to patrolling the back alley. 'Let the buggers just try advancing with their bulldozers!' she shouted to the neighbours. 'We must all stand together against the invaders!' She was promptly joined by the coalman, two snotty-nosed kids, a scabby mongrel and two old women. Then it poured with rain and they all ran for shelter.

Lucky hasn't come back. I do miss him. Three days now since little Tom had an accident. He's taken to playing hopscotch outside on the pavement, and already he's had three fights with the boy from the tripe shop. The first was when the boy tried to pinch his rubber duck. The second was when Tom smacked him on the side of the head with it. I've explained to the little monster that when one loses at hopscotch, one must take it graciously, not swing one's rubber duck at the opponent. The third fight occurred when Tom won and the boy knocked him over.

I hadn't realized, until I took Wilhelmina to see her new school, that until today I had not set foot out of the house, except to scrub the yard and outside lavatory. I don't know who was the more nervous, Wilhelmina or I. It was like running the gauntlet as I hurried down that street, clutching madam in one hand and a shopping bag in the other. It seemed as if every woman in Casey's Court had stepped outside her front door to take stock of us, and not one of them intended to let us go without passing the time of day. As we were already late, I was in a hurry, but remembering their kindness on the night we arrived I could do nothing other than listen while they chatted on. It surprised me to find that I was actually responding. Strange how I began to feel relaxed, when there never seemed time before to stop and pass the time of day with my neighbours. I do believe I could actually enjoy this slower pace of life.

'Settlin' in all right, are ye, lass?' asked one.

'Shouldn't wonder if ol' Pops's ghost still creeps about yon 'ouse!' said another.

'Ye've got some right randy buggers livin' next door, tha' knows!' warned a huge roll of a woman.

'Oh, aye!' rejoined the little wimp beside her. 'But yer won't be bothered wi' them fer a while yet, lass . . . they're away till Sat'day. Gone to see 'er mam in Scotland, I believe.'

One rather ancient and withered old man with a crooked stick and an even more crooked back warbled, 'Yoom *posh* folks, ain't yer? Yer'll not last long round these 'ere parts . . . not all that partial to *posh* folks, isn't Casey's Court.' When I expressed my sincere hope that he might be wrong and we would be accepted by one and all, he brandished his crooked stick at me and shouted, 'Piss off out on it! We don't want you foreigners wi' yer funny talk. Go on! Piss off, I tell yer!'

I was proud of the way I managed to keep my cool. But madam was quite upset. '*You* piss off!' she shouted, and would have kicked him in the shins if a large and prominent breast hadn't thrust itself in front of the old fellow. Attached to it was a slim strawberry blonde with wide dark brown eyes and a rasping voice.

'Now just stop that, Grandad Pitts!' she told him, afterwards smiling at me and saying, 'Ol' Pops were me pa-in-law's best mate, d'yer see? 'E took it real bad when they found 'im flat out in the lavvy.'

'Them buggers did it,' the old fellow shouted, beginning to shake his crooked stick about, 'them posh buggers fro' the council! They want all on us out o' Casey's Court, so's they can knock it down an' build 'ouses fer posh folk!'

'No, Grandad!' the blousy young woman told him in a firm, patient voice. 'I've told yer afore, they just want to modernize Casey's Court, that's all.' She took him back inside. But not before she introduced herself as Sonya and asked whether she could pop round tomorrow for a chat. I agreed reluctantly. She seemed nice, she was about my age, and she had one of those open friendly faces that made you feel welcome. But her appearance! I've only ever seen something similar on the television, in The Bill, when they brought a young woman in for soliciting in the street. Make-up you could scrape off, a cleavage that was positively indecent, and a tiny skirt that left nothing to the imagination. The heels of her shoes must have been at least four inches high, and her legs (which I have to admit were quite shapely) were covered in brown artificial tan – I knew it wasn't a real suntan because on her knees it was much thicker in the skin-creases, and there was a creamy line along the hem of her mini-skirt where it had rubbed against her legs. While I was discreetly taking her measure, she was eyeing me up and down until, with a giggle and without any sarcasm whatsoever, she told the old fellow, 'Yer right though, luv . . . she *is* a posh cow, ain't she!'

Before we emerged from Casey's Court we'd been dragged into her house by one woman to look at her racing-pigeons, another had told us her life story and gone on at great length and in the goriest detail about how 'they've took 'alf of me insides away', and I'd had six

31

pint mugs of tea forced down me, together with two cold pies and a huge helping of upside down pudding. Wilhelmina made a pig of herself and got tummy-ache. And when we got to the school it was closed and everyone had gone home.

But there was one wonderful consolation – we found Lucky! He was sitting at the bus-stop with a huge grey poodle on one side and a fierce-looking bulldog on the other. I couldn't decide whether they were his girlfriends or his minders. When we made our way back to Casey's Court we might have looked a sorry bunch – Lucky all bedraggled and footsore and Wilhelmina still green in the face – but somehow, things didn't seem so bad after all.

Saturday, August 8th

I'm getting quite used to Tom having clean pants! Wilhelmina played out all day with freckle-faced Winnie and, between the two of us, Maggie and I have just about scrubbed and polished every square inch of this little house. It's quite surprising how cosy it's beginning to look. Maggie brought home some flowery curtains and a rug to put in front of the fire. The lovely old grate is an absolute picture, now it's been black-leaded and polished. And there's a pleasant shade of beige distemper beneath all that grime we took off the walls. Lucky seems at home and things look altogether brighter. Thank you, God.

Maggie got in a state today when the phone rang. I was outside on the loo and she came running out in a panic. 'It's the phone!' she cried. 'The phone's ringing!' I told her to go back and answer the blessed thing. When I came into the house, though, she had the receiver upside down and held at arm's length. 'It's bloody useless!' she said, slamming it back down. 'Can't make head nor tail of it!'

I was amazed. Maggie always seems so organized and fearless. 'It won't hurt you,' I told her. I could see she was shaking. 'Good grief, Maggie! Where have you been that you don't know how to use a phone?' She mumbled something about never needing them, then she put on her coat and stormed out. I hope we didn't make a mistake having that phone connected.

I wondered whether Sonya might come as she promised, but she didn't. I wasn't sure whether to be glad or sorry.

Maggie turned up later with a present: a toaster. When we tried it out it sent one piece flying in the air, where it did three somersaults and a back flip and ended up in the sink. The other piece went whizzing under the table and caught Lucky up the rear end. He yelped, shot forward and cracked his head on the table-leg. Now he won't come out. (I reckon he thinks I gave him a kick for going missing.) Little Tom thinks it's all a game, and he's throwing things back at the toaster.

After the children were washed and in bed, Maggie and I had a long chat. She told me that her money was nearly gone. And I told her about my idea regarding the barber's parlour.

'Let's open it again!' I suggested. After all, it had earned old Pops a living, and cutting men's hair couldn't be all that difficult. Across the neck, round the ears – nothing to it.

She thought it was a good idea, so now I've got to decide how to go about it.

Sunday, August 9th

Had a wonderful dream last night! Michael Douglas (son of Kirk) took me out for a meal in a fantastic London restaurant. Afterwards, we went on to a night club where we floated across the dance-floor, lost in each other's arms, his handsome green eyes gazing longingly into mine. Now and then he'd touch the nape of my neck with his long, slim fingers, sending a delicious thrill up my spine and turning my legs to jelly. In the early hours he murmured into my ear, 'Are you ready, my darling?' When we got to his bedroom, I was trembling from head to toe. And when he took me in his arms and kissed me long and passionately, I was like putty in his hands. 'You're so lovely,' he whispered, his sensuous gaze never leaving my face. As he undressed, I grew more and more excited, until with a sort of Tarzan cry he launched himself through the air towards me, arms outstretched. The last thought that rushed through my mind was, 'This will be a night to remember!'

Then he landed on top of me! There was an almighty crash, and I screamed and opened my eyes to see Maggie bending over me, trying to disentangle me from the bed-springs. 'Gave me a bloody fright, you did!' she said, none too pleased. 'The bed's collapsed. What you been up to, eh?' I felt a complete fool. Michael Douglas, I'll never forgive you!

As if I wasn't exhausted enough, it was like World War Three in our scullery this morning. Slices of bread flew in all directions, Maggie went berserk with the yard-broom and broke the lampshade, and little Tom was screaming and diving between everybody's legs. Lucky forgot to duck his rear end and a crusty slice caught him a nasty karate chop right between the danglers. 'Look,' shouted

Wilhelmina, falling about in hysterics, 'Lucky's got one up the arse!' Well, I couldn't believe my ears! I'm afraid I had to smack her, and now she's giving me the silent treatment.

Monday, August 10th

Maggie knew what a state I was in (my nerves really are going) so she packed a few sandwiches and took the monsters to some park or other that freckle-faced Winnie had volunteered to show them.

Sonya paid me a visit – a long one. I'd finished the housework and was savouring the peace and quiet after taking two headache pills when a voice came through the letter-box. 'Yoohoo! It's only Sonya come to see yer.'

I hadn't fully realized before just how well-endowed she is. When I opened the door and she straightened up, I was fortunate not to be sent reeling. As it was, they caught me a glancing blow and nearly lifted me off my feet. 'Sorry, luv,' she said, grinning from ear to ear. 'I ain't got no control over 'em, d'yer see?' I couldn't help but see!

Three hours she stayed. When she swung her way up the passage and out of the door, I was glad to see the back of her – although I asked her to call again, and I meant it. Sonya Pitts may be a loud, raucous bottle-blonde of the kind favoured by the Vernon Jollys of this world, but she is warm-hearted, affectionate and gener-ous, and I'm convinced she's going to be a genuine and much-loved friend to this family. She's not a lady you can take in small doses, either, because when she'd wedged herself into the armchair in the tiny parlour her physical presence was overwhelming. She has a loud booming laugh and a voice that would make an army sergeant tremble. She also has an unnerving habit of waving her arms about to exaggerate her every word. Twice she caught Lucky round the ear, until he had the good sense to realize it was safer beneath the sideboard. 'Poor little bugger!' she commented on seeing two frightened eyes peeping up at her. 'I expect 'e's afeared o' the ghost, ain't 'e?'

'Ghost? What ghost?' I asked, hoping I'd misheard.

'Eeh! Yer don't mean ter tell me ol' Pops ain't paid yer a visit yet?' She stared at me hard, her pretty hazel eyes big and astonished. 'Me an' me big mouth! I've put the fear o' God up yer now, ain't I?' However did she guess? 'There ain't one manjack in Casey's Court who ain't come up agin ol' Pops at one time or another. Oh aye! 'E's often jumped out to sceer a body 'alf to death of a dark night! One poor ol' dear saw the ol' bugger swinging naked fro' a lamp-post – middle o' winter it were, an' ol' Pops wi'out a bloody stitch on! Well, the sight o' some'at she'd forgotten wi' 'er youth fair took the ol' dear's breath away. She ain't never been the same since. An' d'yer mean ter tell me as yer ain't 'eard a strange moanin' noise – kinda low and eerie, like?'

'No, not a sound,' I whispered.

She shook her short blonde locks and clapped her hands together. 'Bugger me, Jessy,' she shouted, 'yer will! I reckon ol' Pops is just bidin' 'is time. Still, now yer know, yer'll be ready fer 'is ol' tricks, won't yer, eh?'

I was shivering in my shoes, but the whole thing seemed to be a great and wonderful source of amusement to her. It didn't take me long to get a grip on myself, though, when I'd had time to think about it. This was *me*! Jessica Jolly, a staunch no-nonsense type who had no time for such silly ideas. Ghosts? Never! 'There are no such things as ghosts.'

Sonya gave out such a roar of laughter and threw herself about in such a frenzy that I could see the ceiling falling down about our ears at any minute. 'You'll see! Ol' Pops is probably watching us right this bloody minute!' To shut her up, I gave her two wedges of Maggie's cherry cake. It worked for about five minutes, after which she launched into a potted history of Casey's Court and its inhabitants, starting with the information that Grandad Pitts was her father-in-law, her husband having long since deserted them both. 'An' good shuts ter bad rubbish!' she declared, spitting cherry cake everywhere. Really! But she did mean well, I knew.

When I finally closed the door behind Sonya, I knew that Casey's Court had been built about a hundred years ago, and that the surrounding streets had been demolished to make way for a new estate. Because of aggressive opposition from Casey's Court residents (most of whom had been born and brought up here) the fate of one of the last remaining relics of Victorian times had been postponed again and again. There were some councillors who went along with residents in their belief that Casey's Court was an important historical landmark and should be modernized rather than demolished. But there were others who saw it as a stumbling-block to their forward visions of wide open spaces and better houses for all. The discussions were heated and ongoing. And, according to Sonya, 'If one bulldozer pokes its nose in 'ere, we'll *ave* the bugger! An' to 'ell wi' the consequences! We'll march on the town hall! We'll barricade us-selves in Casey's Court, an' we'll starve if we 'ave to!' So enthused was I that when she asked 'Ye'll fight alongside us, won't yer, Jessy?' my answer surprised even me.

'Just let them try putting us out,' I said. 'Maggie and I will soon show them the door!'

Sonya gave me a run-down on the residents of Casey's Court, pointing out the ones to avoid and the ones who were 'the salt of the earth'. There was Millie 'Magpie', known as such because of her passion for collecting bright shiny objects. 'You'll like her,' Sonya told me, 'so long as yer 'ide everythin' as glitters!' Then there was Granny Grabber, who, according to Sonya, ''as this fascination fer folks' arses! She'll pinch 'em all . . . man, woman or child. Then she'll swear blind 'tweren't 'er. Oh, an' watch out fer Mad Aggie! She often teks it in 'er 'ead ter march up an' down the street at all 'ours, swearin' an' shoutin' . . . sometimes drunk as a lord, other times just feelin' cantankerous.' I began to wonder whether I'd landed amongst heathens.

As Sonya was going out of the door, she suddenly remembered one other I might like to keep an eye out for. 'Smelly Kelly,' she chuckled. 'Ain't 'ad a wash since VE day, an' stinks to 'igh 'eaven! Yer'll be all right though, Jessy lass . . . if yer keep down wind of 'im!' And Sonya swung her bosom away up the street, tottering on those ridiculously high heels and calling behind her, 'I'd best go an' tell Grandad Pitts yer one of us. It's just as well, 'cause 'e 'ad you down as one o' the enemy.'

I returned to the parlour, exhausted and with a throbbing headache. 'You'd best not toy with me, old Pops,' I told the empty air, 'else you'll rue the day!' Then I felt a fool. Fancy talking to myself. There's no ghost here, of course there isn't.

As I lie here writing this diary, I find myself straining my ears at every sound. I must *not* get nervous. I must *not* listen to silly tales. And from now on I will *not* sleep with my head under the bedclothes. Nor will I behave like a coward, diving upstairs first and shouting, 'Last one to bed can turn out the lights!'

Tuesday, August 11th

Two letters arrived today. One was from Tiffany, saying she didn't much like the look of her new neighbours. Apparently they had the nerve to draw up in a three-year-old car, and there was no indication whatsoever that they might invite the neighbours to a barbecue. To top it all, it appeared that the wife actually *worked*! 'Not our sort at all, Jessica!' Tiffany was most upset. As for me, well, I began to see what a shallow and unfulfilling existence was led by the Tiffanys and Jessica Jollys of this world. And, surprisingly enough, the prospect of ever returning to it was not a pleasant one. It's strange how we live by the standards and values created by our environment and our own insatiable greed. Always rushing about and surrounding ourselves with the latest hi-fi, remote-controlled videos and the fastest, most expensive car. Whatever happened to consideration and compassion for those less fortunate than ourselves? How many real friends did I have down south? Not many, I knew, or they wouldn't have so quickly disappeared with the arrival of my troubles. And what about Tiffany? Whom had she got to turn to within her circle? Recent experiences had left me asking questions, and I didn't care too much for the answers. Tiffany hoped I was managing to stay sane in 'that dreadful place'. And she hoped I would understand if she did not come to visit, at least for a while. Her letter ended on a note of deeper horror. The woman who had escaped from the nearby asylum had not yet been recaptured; the reports described the woman as being 'not immediately dangerous, but unpredictable'. She had escaped with a considerable sum of money from the office safe. 'Of course, I make doubly sure that the doors and windows are securely bolted,' Tiffany wrote. 'Can you *imagine* what might happen if that demented creature came face to face with me?' My sympathy would be with the 'demented creature'!

The second letter was most unexpected and decidedly more pleasant. It was from the solicitor, and contained a cheque for £2,000, being 'the remainder after all accounts were settled'. So the house and everything in it had gone. All bridges were burned and there was no turning back. In a peculiar way, I felt greatly relieved – in fact, I decided on a celebration. Maggie, the two monsters and myself went off to gorge ourselves in the little Chinese restaurant in the town centre. It was midnight when we got home, two A.M. when Tom woke up, sick as a horse, half past four when Maggie ran out to the lavatory, and eight in the morning when we'd all been and were queuing up to go again. I got the feeling it was Vernon Jolly having the last laugh.

When we were ready to troop back indoors, we found the door shut tight against us. After a lot of moaning and complaining, Tom was pushed through the open fanlight above the door, only to call out from inside, 'I can't open the door. It's bolted!'

There followed a deal of arguing as to how the bolt could possibly be on. It certainly couldn't have slipped, because, being old and badly rusted, it took all of Maggie's considerable strength each night to hammer the thing home. But it *is* bolted!' protested Tom from inside, and there seemed nothing for it but to persuade him to climb up and open a window. He was having none of it; 'You're trying to kill me!' he shouted. However did he guess?

My efforts to coax Wilhelmina through the fanlight were not received very well either – she locked herself in the lavatory, every now and then calling out, 'I've a good mind to report you to the cruelty to children people.'

'Enough of this!' declared Maggie. '*I'll* go! I'm an old hand at squeezing in and out of places – if anybody can get in through that fanlight and open the bloody door, I can!'

I never really knew what pandemonium was until now. It's being locked out of your own house, standing in the back yard in your nightie with the wind whistling up your nether regions, one brat locked in the lavatory broadcasting to the world what a cruel parent you are, and your aged bossy mother-in-law well and truly jammed in the fanlight, with her bum bared to the world and the brat inside throwing tomatoes at her!

Within twenty minutes, half of Casey's Court had barricaded themselves in, convinced that the Council had started an invasion. The other half had congregated in our back yard, some armed with ladders, some with all manner of useless advice, and Grandad Pitts brandishing an air-rifle. 'Yer *are* bloody troublemakers! I knew it all along!' In his excitement he squeezed the trigger. The pellet found its way to Maggie's rear end, and she shot through that fanlight like greased lightning and fell like a sack of potatoes right on top of Tom. At least it shut *him* up.

Once inside the house, Sonya managed to lift our spirits by looking about with big scary eyes. 'I told yer ol' Pops was bidin' 'is bloody time, didn't I, eh? 'Appen ye'll believe in ghosts now.'

What nonsense! I'm only sleeping in Maggie's bed because she's shaken up.

Maggie was more shaken up than I realized. Three times in the night, I woke to find her running about with her tin hat on, shouting, 'Rally the troops! Rally the troops!'

The monsters seemed to have recovered from their escapade, because they played out all day and weren't a bit of trouble. I can't help feeling there's a storm brewing.

After they'd been washed and put to bed, Maggie was sufficiently recovered for me to tackle her with a few plans I'd been churning over in my mind. 'I'm serious about re-opening old Pops's barber-shop,' I told her, at which she rightly pointed out that I had no experience of barbering. At this point, Sonya appeared.

'Go on! Open the barber-shop, gel, 'cause yer'll do very well. Folks round 'ere were right sorry when ol' Pops cut 'is last short back an' sides . . . the men 'ave ter go all the way into town fer the nearest barber's now.' She, like me, was excited at the prospect. 'Believe it or not, *I'm* some'at of a dab 'and at giving a short back an' sides!'

'Honestly?' I asked, hoping she wasn't pulling my leg.

'Aye! I'm tellin' yer, afore I were wed, I spent a few years in a barber-shop out Rochdale way. I'll teach yer!'

'And I can keep the appointments book,' offered Maggie, suddenly enthused. 'I can do the ordering and take the money!'

'We *will*!' I fetched the remains of Maggie's sherry and three glasses from the sideboard. I felt really excited, a new woman. 'We'll do it!' And then we heard a clattering noise from the front parlour. When we summoned enough courage to creep in and investigate, it was to see both chairs spinning round on their axles.

'It's ol' Pops showin' 'is approval of yer idea!' Sonya declared, whereupon we filled our glasses, raised them to old Pops, and promised, 'We'll make it the best barber-shop in the whole of Lancashire!'

Thursday, August 13th

The news spread through Casey's Court like wildfire. All day there have been folks knocking on the door, making all sorts of encouraging comments.

'Eeh, that's right grand.'

'Just what we need.'

'Tha'd best 'urry up wi' it,' declared another, taking off his flat cap and displaying his few remaining tufts, ''else it'll be too late fer me!'

Mrs Parkinson from number twelve put another idea to me. 'Will yer be cutting just the men's 'air,' she said, 'or will yer also trim the little lads'? Old Pops never would – said they fidgeted too much. But I'm tellin' yer, Mrs Jolly, there's a bit o' brass ter be made, 'cause there's more little lads round Casey's Court than there are big 'uns!' I told her that we would be catering for the youngsters as well. In for a penny, in for a pound!

Friday, August 14th

It's been one of those days! The monsters have been at each other's throats since they woke up this morning. Lucky's gone missing, and Maggie's in a funny mood – she's taken up two flagstones in the back yard and dug a great hole. 'Never know when you might need to hide,' she retorted when I tackled her about it.

Sonya and I got to work on old Pops's equipment. We

shone his clippers and scissors, we polished the hand-mirrors and basins. We repainted the walls in pastel green, then washed the window and put up a new white blind I bought in town this morning. When everything was ready, we designed a big placard which read:

Pops Barber-shop
Re-opening on Wednesday, August 19th
Haircuts £2.00
Shampoo £1.00
Blow-dry £1.00
Styling £4.00
(Any other request to be negotiated)

We hung the placard in the window and congratulated ourselves on a job well done. 'That'll fotch the buggers in!' laughed Sonya. Hope she's right.

Grandad Pitts was the first caller. 'Yer ain't cuttin' *my* bloody 'air!' he said, brandishing his air-rifle. 'Yer might fool some o' these silly buggers i' Casey's Court, but yer don't fool me. I know yer a Council spy, an' I've got me eyes on yer!'

'Piss off 'ome, Grandad!' Sonya told him. 'She'd 'ave a bloody job to cut your 'air, any road! You're bald as a coot under that flat cap!' He went off muttering at what the world was coming to when his own kith and kin had joined the enemy camp.

I had a quiet word with Sonya about using unnecessary bad language. 'Away wi' yer!' she told me. 'It's what folks round 'ere is used to. Yer'll be using it yerself afore long!'

'What? Never!'

She roared with laughter. 'You'll see!'

I said an extra prayer tonight – I told God that as it was he who'd put me in this predicament my moral welfare was his concern. And he mustn't shirk his responsibility.

Saturday, August 15th

Lucky turned up this morning, and by the look on his face, together with the half ton of dirt clinging to his coat, he'd been up to no good. I gave him a little lecture on how gentlemen should behave. I told him about lady dogs with loose morals and unhealthy appetites. I warned him about the perils of keeping company with wanton females who were only after his body. At tea-time he went missing again.

Wilhelmina stayed in bed all day, whining about her upset tummy. I must admit, though, she didn't look at all well. But it didn't stop her from wading through two pounds of bananas. She must have crept down the stairs every time my back was turned, because after the bunch had noticeably diminished I began counting them. Every time I came back into the parlour, there was one less. She adamantly denied taking them, but *somebody* took them, and if it wasn't Wilhelmina who was it? Tom was under my feet everywhere I went, and Maggie was busy digging her bolt-hole. I do hope Wilhelmina isn't adding lying to her other considerable vices. It is curious, though, because a thorough search of Wilhelmina's bedroom failed to unearth numerous banana skins. 'I expect you think I ate *them* as well!' madam pouted, and I quite think she did. She'd do anything to get one over on me.

Sunday, August 16th

I think I'm buckling under the pressure! I've had the most terrible day. It started at two o'clock this morning, when I was woken by Maggie bending over my bed with eyes like saucers and hair standing bolt upright in petrified clusters beneath her tin hat. When, in response to her prodding and shaking, I wrenched open my weary eyes, I would also have opened my mouth to give her a piece of my mind. But, clamping her hand over my face, she whispered, 'Sssh! There's somebody trying to get in the front door. Listen!'

She was right! There were scratching sounds coming from outside, and the occasional gentle clatter, like the letter-box being tampered with. 'Don't you worry!' Maggie assured me, as I attempted to slither back under the clothes. 'He'll not get in this house, because I'll knock the bugger senseless first!' I thought I'd allow Maggie the chance to become a hero – after all, she was much better equipped than I to deal with intruders, what with her teeth out, that ridiculous tin hat rammed over her ears, and a grimace on her face fit to ward off all evil. But Maggie was not of the same mind. 'Here,' she said, dragging me out of the bed and thrusting a brick into my fist. 'If the blighter comes at you, swipe him with this! Don't miss, mind,' she warned, a look of horrible fore-boding shaping her features, 'because if you don't get him first go you'll not get a second, my girl! He'll be at your throat before you can take aim!' She must have antici-pated my intention to crawl under her bed, because in a minute she'd got me by the scruff of the neck and was propelling me out of the bedroom and down the dark narrow stairs. 'Sssh! Our best chance is to surprise him,' she whispered, as we crept up the passageway. 'You take a little peep through the letter-box, and I'll get ready to fling open the door.'

As long as I live, I'll never forget the fright I had when I gingerly lifted that letter-box. Everything happened so quickly. At first, I couldn't see anything at all. Then two vivid green eyes were staring at me, and a warm hairy

46

hand grabbed my fingers and wouldn't let go! I screamed and screamed, but still the eyes glared at me and my fingers were gripped tight. 'Bloody hell!' shouted Maggie, flinging the door open and hurling her brick into the pitch blackness. There came a terrible scream and a body fell into the passageway on top of us. Suddenly every light down Casey's Court was on, with all and sundry out on the street in their nightwear, running in different directions and shouting things like 'Jesus, Mary an' Joseph, is there a murder or what?' Maggie fled into the street shouting 'Rally the troops! Rally the troops!' and Grandad Pitts ran at me with his air-rifle.

'I knew it, yer buggers!' he screamed. 'Just like your sort to launch a night-attack!' I do believe he would have shot me there and then, if Sonya hadn't appeared in a flowing white tent, risking life and limb with every frantic step as her charlies bounced up and down within an inch of her chin.

'Yer gormless fart!' she shouted, grabbing hold of the little fellow and swinging him round. 'Gerroff indoors afore I do yer a bloody injury!' She did the same to Maggie, and in a matter of minutes she had the situation under control. I'm ashamed to say I was useless, shivering like a jelly and rooted to the spot, the body still prostrate at my feet.

Sonya examined the lifeless form. 'Well, I'm buggered!' she said, throwing back her head and giving out a roar like thunder. 'It's Mad Aggie!'

'Mad Aggie?' I couldn't stop trembling. 'Is she dead?'

'Naw, she ain't dead. Pissed as a newt is what she is!' She pointed to the figure, which began coughing and spluttering. 'I'd best get the silly ol' fool off 'ome!'

I quickly explained what had happened. 'She was staring through the letter-box at me – two vivid green

eyes,' I said, 'and then she grabbed me. It was horrible
. . . her hand was all hairy.'

'Away wi' yer, yer silly arse!' Sonya was most amused.
'Mad Aggie's eyes ain't green! They're a sort of muddy
brown, on account o' they're allus bloodshot. An' look at
them 'ands.' She lifted one of the small limp wrists.
'Them's no more 'airy than Grandad Pitts's bald pate!'
She shook her head. 'You an' Maggie must 'a been sharin'
the same nightmare . . . ain't that right, Maggie?' she
called to my mother-in-law, who had retreated to the far
end of the passage and was looking sheepish, a monster
on each side of her. When she gave no answer, Sonya
laughed. 'Aw, don't worry yerselves over it. I'll see to this
'un. You get yerselves back to bed.' Then she hoisted the
figure over her shoulders and, with a promise that she'd
look in first thing in the morning, she was away up the
road. 'Oh, by the way, yer neighbours is back the
morrow,' she called. 'Yer'll 'ave to get used ter bumps in
the night *then*!' The whole street echoed with her raucous
laughter as she disappeared from sight.

Sonya was right about those young neighbours. They
arrived about half past eleven, and the house has been
shaking on its foundations ever since. And such noises!
Grunting and groaning and intermediate rattling. 'I feel
better now,' piped up Wilhelmina. 'Can I go and play
with them next door?'

'No, you can't!' The very idea! 'You go and play with
Tom.' She pointed out that it sounded as if they were
'having more fun' next door. I didn't know what to say.

Trust us to get squashed between exhibitionist neighbours and another on the other side who hasn't shown her
face yet. According to Sonya, she's 'a funny little sort, is
Larkin. Likes ter keep well away from folk, because of
'er affliction.' When I asked what affliction, Sonya

48

laughed out loud, saying, 'When Larkin gets used ter yer she'll show 'erself . . . and then yer'll be in no doubt as to 'er affliction!' I'm not sure I want to know any more.

Monday, August 17th

I had a visitor today. I'm ashamed to say that my first impression of him quite caught me off my guard. He was the most gorgeous, handsome, sensuous and sexy hunk I've seen in years (more than a bit like Michael Douglas). The only thing is, he's also hateful, arrogant, selfish, vain, and a typical chauvinistic pig!

I was on my own when he came to the door. Maggie had taken the monsters from under my feet down to that little park, which was just as well, because the way they were behaving there was every chance I'd throttle the pair of them with my bare hands. Thus, at half past eleven, covered in flour and wearing a most unglamorous pinny, I opened the door to see a tall, dark vision of manhood smiling at me – the most devastatingly beautiful smile! He even had a delicious little dimple in his chin – just like Kirk Douglas.

'Hello,' he murmured, in velvety tones, his handsome black eyes clinging to me and sending me weak at the knees, 'are you Jessica Jolly? New owner of Pops Barbershop?' As I nodded, dumbfounded, it crossed my mind how elegant he was. He had a lean and hungry physique, and was dressed in dark green cords, casual white shirt and well cut brown jacket. He had on a green-check flat cap and, set at a jaunty angle on that longish, thick black hair, it suited him – made him look sort of devil-may-care. From his accent, he was definitely a native of these parts. And, from his manner, he definitely knew how to get the better of a woman.

After I'd invited him in (and dashed upstairs to give myself a once-over, renew the make-up and put on my most fetching frock) it soon became obvious what he was after. Unfortunately, it wasn't me.

'I'm Barny Singleton,' he introduced himself, 'and as most of the Casey's Court residents come to my barber's shop, since old Pops closed down, it would seem that you and I are set to be rivals in business.' You could have knocked me down with a feather. Then I could have knocked *him* down when he made a certain suggestion (probably because it wasn't the one I would have preferred). 'A vital, attractive young woman like you shouldn't be tying yourself to long weary hours in a barber's shop.' (Oh, those black devilish eyes! The way they promised things . . . if you know what I mean.) 'I'm sure, with a figure like yours and that flaming red hair, you'd be far more suited to modelling, or something of that nature.' (The cunning swine!) 'Why don't you let me pay you a good price for old Pops's stuff, eh? I've got all the most up to date equipment, of course, so I don't really need it . . . but I'm willing to take it off your hands.' He smiled that devastating smile. 'I expect, like old Pops, it's run its time out, eh?' No sooner were the words out of his mouth than the house was filled with a terrible moaning sound, like wind through the tree-tops. 'Good Lord, what's that?' he exclaimed, raising his eyebrows. 'Sounds like you've got a draught up your chimney.' Then, with a laugh, he said, 'It's probably old Pops telling me off for running his equipment down . . . he always did have a lot to say for himself, did old Pops!' Whereupon his chair was flung sideways as one of the legs disappeared through a hole in the floor (a hole, I might add, which was not there when I ran our new second-hand hoover round this morning). Getting to his feet, he lifted the chair to safer ground. 'These old houses are way past their prime,' he said. 'The Council's quite right to consider demolishing them. If they leave it much longer, the whole lot will fall round our ears like a pack of cards.'

'Not *your* ears, surely?' I had no idea he lived in Casey's Court.

''Fraid so. I live with my young son across the way – so I have a wonderful view of that most artistic placard you put in the window.' He was looking at me in that particular way. I could feel my knees going, so I thought it best to show him the way out. 'I'm so pleased to have made your acquaintance, Mr Singleton . . .'

'Barny, please.'

'Mr Singleton,' I insisted. 'I have no intention of parting with old Pops's equipment. I shall need it all when the customers start flooding in.'

'Oh? Tell me, Jessica, have you any experience?'

My heartbeat steadied when I realized he meant experience in barbering. 'Of course!' I lied. 'Now, if you'll excuse me, some of us have work to do.'

On the way up the passage he paused at the front parlour, and seeing how Sonya and I had made the place gleam he commented, 'Well, it certainly *looks* very professional.' He turned round so quickly that I wasn't expecting it, so, when his dark teasing eyes burned down into mine with a warm smile, it took all of my self-control not to pounce on him and drag him into the back parlour. He'll never know what pleasures he missed, though, because his next words brought out the fighting spirit in me. What he said was, 'I admire your guts, Jessica Jolly, and if things were different I'd back you to the hilt. But, first and foremost, I'm a businessman. I've invested a great deal of time and money in my venture' – he smiled knowingly – 'and, unlike you, I *am* fully experienced. I think it's only fair to warn you here and now that I've no intention of seeing you poach any of my customers. I'll fight you tooth and nail!'

I recovered enough to rush to the door and call after him, 'Do your damnedest, Singleton! You don't frighten me!' Then I went back inside and kicked the sideboard. Who did he think he was? I was so enraged that as I paced up and down I completely forgot the hole in the floor.

When Sonya came in a few minutes later, I was hopping about in agony. 'Just you 'ang on,' she told me. 'I'll be back in a minute.' She was, and she brought a bottle of witch-hazel with her. Marvellous stuff. It took the bruise out of my ankle in no time.

When I told her what had happened (she'd seen Barny Singleton leaving) she threw her arms above her head and roared, 'What! The cheeky bugger! Just let 'im try an' stop us, that's all! I 'ope yer told 'im straight, told 'im ter piss off!' She gave me a funny look. 'Yer didn't let the bugger melt yer wi' them dark sexy eyes of 'is, did yer?' she demanded (ready, I'm sure, to give me a good shaking).

'No, I did not!'

She dived at me and dug me in the ribs with her elbow. 'I wouldn't 'a blamed yer, though,' she chuckled. ''E's bloody gorgeous, ain't 'e? Sends me into a tizzy every time I claps eyes on 'im. What I couldn't do fer that one is nobody's business!'

I knew just how she felt, and the sight of Sonya drooling over him put my guard up against Barny Singleton. 'From now on we regard him as the enemy. Barny Singleton has declared war. And if that's the way he wants it, that's the way he'll get it.'

We went through all the ways he could possibly inter-fere with us, and we came to the conclusion that there was nothing whatsoever he could do to prevent us from starting business. We parted, with Sonya promising to spend all tomorrow afternoon showing me the rudiments of barbering. I also found out that Barny Singleton was thirty-six and had been divorced these past four years. He had a son about Tom's age.

Tuesday, August 18th

Coming up north has had a bad effect on Lucky. He's taken to staying out till all hours, and every morning now there's a string of straggly hussies waiting in the back alley for him. He's got so wayward he doesn't listen to a thing I say. I've done my duty and I can do no more. I've warned him about the error of his ways. I've told him that if he insists on cocking his leg over every likely looking female he'll end up going the way of Vernon Jolly. I've banned black pudding from his diet. Just the look of it could be giving him ideas.

Maggie's taken to spouting politics since some lout in the park called her an old trout. 'This Tory government's got the right idea,' she remarked, wearing her tin hat. 'Teach the buggers respect and make them stand in the corner.' It seems her namesake can do no wrong. She even put pen to paper and told Mrs Thatcher to keep on rapping the knuckles of anyone who disagreed with her. 'Look how well behaved Denis is,' she pointed out. 'It takes years of discipline and self-sacrifice to achieve such standards.' She was adamant that Denis should be held up as an example to all developing manhood.

A dark-haired little boy came knocking at the door this

morning. 'Hello, Mrs Jolly,' he said politely. 'I'm Danny Singleton.' I might have known. He's got the same handsome black eyes and crooked smile. 'Me dad said I could come and play with your Tom . . . if that's all right?'

'Of course,' I told him, thinking at the same time that if Barny Singleton was looking to plant an enemy in the camp he could think again. There'd be nothing said in this household that I wasn't prepared to tell him to his face. In fact, as I told the boy to go through to the back yard where he'd find Tom, I caught sight of his father watching from his front step. I hope he felt duly snubbed when I stuck my nose in the air and banged the door shut. When the crash brought Maggie running from the parlour, I told her the wind had caught it, and these houses *were* falling apart. It was the only way I could explain why the front door was lying on the pavement.

After lunch, when Maggie was snoring in the chair and the monsters were fighting in the back yard, Sonya came round with three long floor-mops. 'Right!' she said. 'We'll start with a short back and sides . . . when yer get that right, I might let yer 'ave a go at doin' a quiff!' When I asked her what a quiff was, she told me not to be so ignorant. 'Get thisel' in yon parlour,' she instructed, 'an' let's 'ave no more silly questions.' I've heard about women who go over the top when put in positions of authority. I do hope Sonya isn't one.

She fussed and fretted until finally she had the mop handle securely trapped down the back of the barber's chair (from the back it looked just like Michael Heseltine sitting there). 'First thing you do, as soon as yer've got yer customer sitting comfortable, is to remove all mirrors, 'cause yer don't want 'im watchin' yer while yer lops off 'is 'air. It's most unnerving. Then yer kind of run yer 'ands over 'is 'ead and stroke it gently – that puts 'em in a good frame o' mind, d'yer see?' When I nodded, she told me to get round to the front where I could see what she was doing (which was more than the mop-head could, smothered as it was by Sonya's monstrous overhang. When I pointed that out, she gave a great guffaw and told me it was a trick of hers to 'keep the buggers' minds off what I'm doing up top, like').

Preliminaries out of the way, Sonya set to with the scissors. I have to say I was astounded. When she'd finished with that mop-head, it looked like one of those film stars in the silent movies, with hair all smart and larded down, and a side parting that looked as if it had been cut with a knife. I was most impressed, and I told her so, although I was foolish enough to mention that it might perhaps be a bit old-fashioned. 'Old-fashioned be buggered!' she said, hitching up her charlies and stepping back to admire her handiwork. 'Yer not down bloody south amongst them poofters now!' I think she felt affronted (she certainly looked it). 'Yer up the bloody north, where men is men, an' they'll not thank you for any o' that bloody mousse nonsense nor curls as dangle down their backs. Naw! You be telled by me as knows. What the fellas round these parts want is a proper 'aircut, an' don't you forget it, my gal!'

Then it was my turn. When I'd finished, Sonya took a long thoughtful look at it from all angles. 'Well, it ain't bad, considering,' she observed, tapping the comb against her teeth as she walked round and round.

I felt quite pleased. 'Considering what?' I asked, and was somewhat deflated when she replied, 'Considering that if that were a fella, yer'd 'a chopped both 'is bloody ears off!'

I must admit, though, that Sonya was very patient with

55

me. The next time it was my turn I only chopped one ear off. 'I'll be all right tomorrow,' I told her, not at all unnerved.

'Yer better 'ad be,' she roared, 'else there's gonna be a few deaf folks in Casey's Court!' Bless her old heart.

I'm so excited about tomorrow and opening up for business, I can't go to sleep. And I've got a funny feeling that old Pops is watching. You know, I'm growing quite fond of the old fellow.

Wednesday, August 19th

Disaster! We heard nothing in the night. But when I opened the door to the barber parlour this morning there was a huge hole in the middle of the floor, into which had slid both chairs and all my ambitions.

I was furious. 'You old bugger, Pops!' I screamed at the walls, shaking my fists and putting all the blame on him. 'I thought you were on my side!' He must have taken umbrage, because everything that wasn't nailed down took flight with a vengeance, all aiming in my direction and intent on doing me bodily harm. 'I don't care!' I shouted, slamming the door. 'You should have kept an eye on things, you silly old fool!' Then I sat in the scullery, bemoaning my fate, while the monsters strapped themselves to the toppled barber chairs, rigged up a mast with the broom, used the brand new white overalls for sails and, oblivious of my shattered dreams, set out to sail the world. I hope they never come back.

Maggie was very supportive, bless her. 'You sit there while I make you a cup of tea and a slice of toast!' she instructed. The fact that she was totally undeterred by her first two efforts with the toaster (which resulted in one slice impaled on the door-knob and the other pursuing Lucky into the back yard) just shows what strength of character the woman has. As for Sonya, who turned up some ten minutes later, ready for work, she was as philosophical as ever.

First of all, she hung up a notice on the front door, telling any would-be customers that the opening had been delayed. Then, slapping me heartily on the back, she said, 'You 'ang on there a minute, Jolly. I'll be back in a minute with just the thing.' She came back with a bottle of gin. 'We'll get pissed,' she said. 'There's nowt else for it.' I hadn't the heart to reprimand her for employing such base language.

Two hours later we hadn't a care in the world. When the monsters rushed in to say there was a man at the door, Sonya shouted, 'Tell the bugger to sod off!'

Maggie went looking for her tin hat, and when I struggled up the passageway to confront the pin-striped blur at the door, saying in my most polite voice 'If you want your hair cut, I'm afraid you'll have to come back next week, because the house is falling down', he thrust a stiff little thing into my hand and said with a sour look (well, I think it was a sour look, but I couldn't be sure because from where I was standing his eyes had drifted down to his chin and his nose was in the middle of his forehead), 'Mrs Jolly, I can assure you that, whether the house is falling down or not, you won't be cutting any-one's hair – not today, not next week – and perhaps not at all, in these premises!'

'Thank you very much,' I said, trying to wow him with one of my most beguiling smiles, which somehow stuck to my face like a leer. 'Would you care to come into the parlour for a cup of gin?'

'I would not!' It was difficult to understand what he was

saying, when his mouth was perched on top of his trilby. 'When you are . . . able, please contact me at that number!' With that he marched away, leaving me still clutching his card.

'Don't think I can't cut your bloody hair!' I shouted after him. 'I have practised on a mop, you know!'

It was tea-time when we all regained our senses. 'I never should 'a let you talk me into fetching that gin,' complained Sonya. Maggie began racing round in circles, shouting 'I'm blind, I'm blind!' until I explained that she'd fallen asleep with her tin hat over her face. Lucky was still trembling in the outside loo, with the slice of toast waiting at the door to get him. Can't think why we ever called him Lucky.

As my brains are somewhat scrambled, I'm having an early night. I'll pick up the pieces tomorrow. (And, dear Lord, forgive me. Not only did I fail to chastise Sonya for using unnecessary language, but I do believe *I* used a swear word on that poor deformed creature who came to the door today.)

Thinking about that bottle of gin which Sonya brought round got me wondering. Where does she get her money from? As far as I can tell, there's only Grandad Pitts's old age pension, and that wouldn't run to extras like gin. Hm – most curious!

Thursday, August 20th

More trouble! The gentleman who called at the door and caught me somewhat inebriated was from the Council. It seems I need to have permission to re-open Pops Barbershop. I can't help feeling that Barny Singleton might have put them up to it. Anyway, I've to fill in all sorts of tiresome forms and have my premises inspected. If anybody in authority saw that parlour now they'd slap a demolition order on it, and no mistake. 'Play for time,' Sonya suggested. Well, I will . . . because I've got no choice. I'm caught between two evils here – I can't afford to have any work done on this crumbling little heap they call a house (which I've come to love) and there's little prospect of my earning money from hairdressing for some time. I've only got fourteen hundred pounds left from the solicitor's cheque, and that won't last for ever.

I went down to the local DHSS office. There was a queue a mile long, and it was two hours before I was attended to – by which time I was familiar with every person in that queue. I felt their every twinge, knew their love-lives in graphic detail, and was even invited to join in a card-game set up in the lobby by some of the more enterprising of them. I won two pounds forty. (The chief clerk did all right, as well – he won six pounds.) When I got to the desk, I was thoroughly interrogated by a great mountain of a woman who leaned across the desk to eye me in closer detail. 'You must display all your assets,' she informed me (she was certainly displaying hers). 'But you can't fill out the form here. If we took the time to fill out every form here we'd never get a thing done!' She drew in such a big weary sigh that her assets were promptly increased to such frightening proportions that everybody in the queue took a step back. 'Take it home. Fill the form in at home.'

'I will,' I assured her, not wanting her to feel the need for another big weary sigh, 'but what are my chances of getting some help from you?'

'You say you own property?'

I half-nodded, because it was, well, half a property.

'You have money from the sale of a previous property'

– I could feel the ship sinking – 'and you intend to open up a business – a hairdresser's?'

'Well . . . sort of. But it's not as simple as all that.'

'It never is!' She gave me an exhilarating smile. 'To be quite honest, Mrs Jolly, I doubt very much whether you're a deserving cause. I'm afraid you'd be well advised to expect no help . . . there are others more in need. Next!' she boomed, leaving me in no doubt that I'd been dismissed. I screwed the form up and threw it in the litter-bin.

It was tea-time when another avenue of possibility presented itself. There came a knock on the door, and when I opened it I saw a tiny woman with a halo of grey hair and bright blue frightened eyes. 'Hello, Mrs Jolly,' she said in a thin little voice, 'I'm Larkin . . . Edna Larkin, from next door.' I suddenly remembered Sonya telling me that the little woman had 'an affliction', but there was no affliction that I could see. 'I'm sorry I haven't introduced myself before . . . but shy I am, d'yer see?' She was going a delicate shade of pink – was that the affliction Sonya had mentioned?

'Oh, you needn't be shy of me, Mrs Larkin,' I assured her. 'I'm very pleased to make your acquaintance.'

'As a rule, I keep myself to myself . . . I have my reasons, dearie. But I was so lookin' forward to havin' my hair done at your barber's . . . and now I understand there's been a delay?' She went on to ask whether I might consider coming in to her parlour 'to give me one o' them curly perms', she said, with a shy smile. 'I've allus fancied one o' them curly hairdos.'

Of course I agreed at once, and it occurred to me that if there was one customer wanting her hair done in the privacy of her own parlour there may be others. When I made that suggestion to her, Larkin made a comment, but I couldn't hear a word of it for the deafening clap of thunder that rent the air. 'Goodness me!' It gave me such a fright that I instinctively ducked. 'Looks like we're in for a bad storm!' I said, still shaking.

Larkin went a vivid shade of scarlet and backed away. ''Tweren't no clap of thunder,' she whispered. 'I am sorry, dearie . . . but me insides is allus full of wind. When it builds up to screaming pitch there's just no controlling it.'

She was close to tears, poor thing, so I assured her she mustn't worry, because we all have one affliction or another. 'Look at me. I've got two – Tom and Wilhelmina.'

She went away quite pleased at the prospect of having her hair done, and, in spite of her 'affliction', I thought she was a sweetheart.

Later, when I told Sonya about it, she laughed out loud. 'She's all right, is Larkin,' she said. 'She takes some stick from a certain few down Casey's Court. An' the kids tease 'er some'at chronic.'

I was shocked and said so. And, when Sonya claimed that some folks blamed 'Larkin's explosions' for weakening their foundations – well! The idea was preposterous. (Although I have to admit I thought it strange that my parlour floor suddenly caved in like that.)

Anyway, thanks to little Larkin, I traipsed round Casey's Court with my appointments book, and acquired three other customers who liked the idea of a visiting hairdresser. Maggie assured me she would keep an eye on the monsters, and Sonya was very pleased for me. It was then that I received another shock. 'You go an' earn yersel' a bob or two,' she said. 'I'll bide me time till yer gets the barber's open.' When I pointed out that I thought she was also hoping to earn a bob or two she roared with laughter. 'I've already got a Bob or two. I've got a Fred an' a Paddy as well.' Seeing my confused expression, she slapped me heartily on the back as she waddled out. 'Only them buggers like a lot more than an 'aircut, luv! I've one comin' tonight as stands there naked while I throw ice-cream dollops at 'im. One good thing, though – 'e ain't fussy about the flavour!'

'You're . . . a *prostitute*?' The word stuck in my throat.

'Aw, no . . . I'm no prostitute.' Sonya was offended. 'I'm a *provider*! That's what I am. I provides a service fer them poor buggers as can't get it elsewhere!'

I still haven't got over what Sonya does for a living. But, somehow, I can't help but like her. She's the most honest, helpful and straightforward person I've ever come across – what might be termed the 'salt of the earth'. (All the same, I don't think I'll tell Maggie just yet.) And I have to smile when I think what Tiffany would say if she knew I was fraternizing with a loose woman.

Friday, August 21st

I went down to the town centre today and bought two perms – one for normal hair and one easy-curl. I also purchased a portable hair-dryer and three plastic caps, together with a few thousand curlers of various sizes, two lather brushes and half a dozen old-fashioned cut-throat scrapers. I intend to branch out into shaves and beard-trims, and I'm a little nervous of mechanical things.

Lucky's gone missing again – he will not be told! On his own head be it.

There was pandemonium here this evening – it quite shook me. It happened about ten thirty, just as Maggie and I decided to call it a night. 'I'll lock up,' Maggie said. 'I doubt if Lucky's coming home now.' No sooner had we got to the bottom of the stairs than it sounded as if all hell was let loose out at the back. We rushed along the alley with a few dozen others, wondering what was going on and ready to fight the world (except Larkin, who stood trembling in her nightgown and cap by the back gate. 'Oh dearie me,' she kept saying, wringing her little hands together, her bright blue eyes all big and terrified, 'dearie, dearie me . . . whatever is it?').

It was Sonya. She'd been enjoying her nightly constitutional in the outside loo when apparently a huge grey rat had scurried past. Not being partial to the creatures, she'd shot backwards with her legs in the air, and inadvertently thrust her very shapely buttocks down the pan! And so jammed tight were they that neither screaming nor wriggling could loosen them. I'm sorry to say that the good folks of Casey's Court doubled up in fits of laughter before seeing what could be done to help Sonya out of her predicament.

'I know just the thing!' Maggie shouted, tearing off at top speed in the direction of the builders' compound. When she came back, armed with an iron crow-bar, Sonya nearly had a fit.

'She's a bloody lunatic!' she shouted, flailing her arms and slipping even further from sight. Hard as I tried to keep a straight face, I'm ashamed to admit I was in hysterics. 'It's all right fer you, yer silly bugger!' she told me, quite rightly. 'It ain't your bloody arse as is wedged like a cork in a bottle!' When, at that point, Maggie advanced with the crow-bar, she grew frantic. 'You come near me wi' that thing an' I'll 'ave yer up fer bloody assault!'

It was just as well that somebody had seen fit to call the fire brigade, because I doubt if Sonya could have been freed any other way. Nevertheless, she didn't take too kindly to being sucked up what she called 'a soddin' sewer-pipe'.

Sunday, August 23rd

Tom's started asking embarrassing questions about his little thing. I told him it's an extra bit God gave him.

That randy young couple next door were at it all night again. All that grunting and panting put the fear of God up poor old Maggie. 'You're not telling me that's normal!' she said, waking me up so I could have a listen. 'There's more going on in there than meets the eye!' (That might be true, because, apart from all those bumps in the night, neither Maggie nor I have seen hide or hair of those two rascals.) When I mentioned it to Sonya, she said, 'Well, you won't, chuck. They both work from dawn to dusk, though nobody knows where. Aye! It is mysterious – but folks round these parts 'ave learned ter mind their own business. Live an' let live, that's what I say. An' if the buggers is enjoyin' themselves, well, more power to their elbows' – she gave one of her raucous laughs – 'an' to any other bits as might get in the way!' She's a character.

Barny Singleton came knocking on the door this evening. When I kept him on the step and asked him to state his business, he swallowed me up in those dark flashing eyes and looked me up and down before saying, 'I came to tell you how sorry I am that you couldn't get the shop open as planned.' Then came the real reason for his visit. 'I'm still in the market for all your equipment – damaged or otherwise.'

'I'll bet you are, Barny Singleton!' I was furious. 'You're not a bit sorry I can't open the business . . . in fact, it was probably you who prayed the floor would fall in!'

'Now, come on, Jessica! All right, I'll admit I'm not sorry! Because it's my belief that there's only room for one barber-shop in this vicinity, and that's mine. But, that aside, I wouldn't wish disaster on you, honestly.' He gave me one of those delicious crooked smiles. 'I'd much rather we got together like intelligent adults and came to some sort of amicable agreement.'

'Are you prepared to shut down your barber's shop?' I asked, suppressing those primeval urges that made me want to swoop on him and tear his clothes off.

'Of course not.'

'Well, neither am I. You can wish hell and damnation on me . . . you can send an *army* of planning officials, and you can bombard me with tempting offers for my equipment, and all you'll get is my promise of an all-out fight. And may the best man win!'

He had the cheek to wink at me. 'You're a real beauty when you're riled,' he said. I blushed, and he smiled deep into my eyes. 'All the same . . . I've no choice but to fight you to the bitter end.' Then he was gone.

'Don't you gi' the bugger an inch!' warned Sonya when I told her. 'You show 'im yer've no intention o' lettin' 'im get the better of yer!' When I asked what she would do, she told me, 'Listen, chuck, 'e can 'ave the better o' me any time 'e wants! But then, I ain't got no axe ter grind.

65

On top o' which, I'm not the sort Barny Singleton would go fer. I'm tellin' you, chuck, the bugger'd 'ave you on a plate any time, given 'alf a chance!' I assured her he would not get the chance (more's the pity).

Little Larkin's quite pleased with her curly perm. 'Oh, Mrs Jolly,' she said, after seeing herself in the mirror, 'I look just like Shirley Temple.' Actually, I was pleasantly surprised it had turned out so well, in spite of the fact that I should have done a strand test first. (Thank God for Superglue! That bald patch at the back of her head will never notice. Bless her, she thought I wanted it to mend my comb.)

Monday, August 24th

I've been at death's door all day. Maggie's been wonderful. The monsters have also been very thoughtful – they stayed away from me.

Sonya says I've picked up a bug. (I think the Lord's calling me, to explain the hash I've made of things.)

Tuesday, August 25th

Still feeling poorly. A huge bouquet of flowers arrived from Barny Singleton. (If he thinks it will win him any favours, he just might be lucky.)

Wednesday, August 26th

I made a real effort today. I got out of bed and took myself down to the parlour. I felt as weak as a kitten, and very sorry for myself, when Sonya arrived. She told me what had happened the previous evening. Apparently, she and one of her clients were having 'a right noisy, enjoyable session' on the kitchen table when in burst Grandad Pitts with his air-rifle. 'The bugger let fly!' related Sonya with horror. 'Peppered Paddy's bare arse like a bloody colander!' When I collapsed in a fit of hysterics, she told me off. ''Tweren't no laughin' matter, I can tell yer, seein' poor Paddy runnin' up the road wi'out 'is trousers, an' that silly ol' bugger chasin' 'im – shoutin' as 'ow the Council ought ter be ashamed, if they thought to win over the women o' Casey's Court wi' a bit of 'ow's yer father.'

'It's just as well Grandad Pitts didn't find out what you were really up to.'

'Oh, aye. There is that,' agreed Sonya, 'but I could 'a done wi'out the hour long lecture 'e gave me afterwards . . . on the birds an' bees.'

Sonya cheered me up no end. I'm feeling much better, and looking forward to the two jobs I've got tomorrow – a perm for Granny Grabber, and a short back and sides for old Mr Twistle.

Lucky turned up. He looks worse than I do.

Thursday, August 27th

When I collected the milk from the step this morning, I saw a gorgeous brunette draw up outside Barny Single-ton's house in a swanky car. As he was getting into it, he called out, 'Good morning, Jessica . . . lovely day.' When I looked up again, he was kissing the creature full on the mouth. I went straight in and threw his flowers in the dustbin.

Maggie's got a black eye. She forgot to duck when the toaster threw another fit.

Tom wants to know if he's the only one in the house who's got 'an extra bit from God'. I told him Lucky was blessed in the same way.

Fred Twistle is an absolute darling. So is his wife, Bertha. They put me in mind of Pinky and Perky – both round and short, both with pink pudding faces, and both full of bright useless information. He's an authority on the mating habits of pigeons – he keeps twenty in the back garden. And what she doesn't know about the common moggy isn't worth knowing – she has four. Between the cats and the pigeons, there's a constant battle, which isn't helped by the fact that Fred's partly deaf and Bertha's a bit of a bossy-boots.

I had something of a battle with Fred's haircut because of his prominent ears (I couldn't forget what I did to the mop-head I practised on). 'I want a nice smart 'aircut, gel!' he said, shooing the cats out of the chair and settling himself comfortably, 'but leave a bit ter cover up me ears, won't yer?'

I was doing fine – I'd done the top and all round his neck, and was very carefully snipping the area round his ear-lobes – when I accidentally trod on one of the marauding cats. It let out a yelp and sprang right past my face to land on Fred's shoulder. 'Get the bloody thing orf!' he shouted, lashing out in all directions. When Bertha retrieved the silly thing, I was horrified to see that I'd lopped a great chunk of hair off above Fred's ear.

''Ere!' He caught sight of himself in the sideboard

mirror. 'Thi can't leave me lopsided like that, gel! I'll be a bloody laughing-stock!' He was not pleased. Bertha said it served him right for frightening the cat.

It was nerve-racking, because the more I straightened up one side, the more uneven looked the other, and I had to go backwards and forwards till both sides matched. When I surveyed the finished result, I was devastated. I couldn't quite decide whether Fred looked more like a bald hedgehog or a geriatric bovver-boy. His own impression was different, though, because when he examined himself in the mirror and took stock of the fact that his ears jutted out some four inches on either side, he screeched, 'Bloody Nora! I look like a Roman urn.' (He did, too.)

'By! I never knew yer 'ad such great lug-'oles!' shouted Bertha gleefully, rolling about in a fit of giggles which appeared to upset him even more, because he rounded on me.

'Call yersel' a bloody 'airdresser, eh? Comin' 'ere fro' the south wi' yer fancy ideas an' terrorizin' us poor innocent folk. 'Ow the 'ell d'yer expect me ter show me face outside that bloody door, eh? What! If I so much as set foot in yon pub, the buggers'll be using me 'ead ter strike their matches on!' (He was upset, poor thing.)

I did my best to pacify him, but he was having none of it. 'Gerrout!' he shouted, ramming his flat cap over his ears. 'Go on! Gerrout!'

'Now then, Fred . . .'tain't right ter talk to Mrs Jolly that way.' At least Bertha was trying to be kind. 'Yer can't blame anybody else fer the size o' yer ears. 'Tain't 'er fault they're so cumbersome.'

He turned a painful colour, picked up his walking-stick, and waved it in the air. 'I'm tellin' yer, if yer norrout that bloody door in ten seconds, I'll flatten yer!' I was out in six.

Granny Grabber lived next door, so I hadn't far to go. At least there wasn't much that could go wrong here, because I'd done a perm before. And Larkin was satisfied. All the same, there was a hastily scribbled note on the door, saying, 'I've gone out, Mrs Jolly. Leave me alone.' She must have heard Fred Twistle shouting. I could see her hiding behind the curtains and peeping out at me.

'All right, Granny Grabber,' I shouted through the letter-box. 'If you change your mind, you know where to find me.' I thought I'd go and have a cup of coffee with Sonya – she'd cheer me up.

When I rattled the knocker, a long barrel was thrust through the letter-box. 'Halt! Who goes there?' came the authoritative voice of Grandad Pitts.

'It's me,' I shouted, 'Jessica. I've come to see Sonya, if you please.'

'Well, yer can't.'

'Why not – is she out?'

'Naw. She ain't out. But she's got this college feller up in 'er room – she's thinkin' o' tekkin' up archery classes.'

'Oh,' I said, not knowing what to think – until there came a 'psst' from above. When I looked up, there was Sonya, hanging out of the window and grinning from ear to ear.

'Sod off, afore 'e gets suspicious,' she told me. 'I'll see yer later.'

It just hasn't been my day!

I found Tom with my tape-measure and, lying nearby, on his back with his legs in the air, was Lucky. 'Tom, what *are* you doing?' I asked.

He looked at me as though I had just crawled out from under a stone. 'Aren't mummies stupid,' he said, with a big patient sigh. 'I'm seeing if Lucky's thing is bigger than mine, of course!' (Of course – silly me!)

Wilhelmina's taken to moaning about the fact that soon the holidays will be over and she'll have to go to school. When she pointed out that freckle-faced Winnie's mam lets her stay at home, I told her it was the duty of a friend to point out to Winnie how much she was missing.

'But Winnie can do what she likes all day!' the monster moaned. 'She can play on her skateboard and go to the pictures – *and* she gets money for ice-cream and sweets.'

'All the same, *you* are going to school!' I had no intention of shirking my responsibility. The fact that she stormed off upstairs and locked herself in her bedroom all day only confirmed that I'd done the right thing. It was absolute bliss. I must think of something else which might have the same effect.

A man came to the door. He was a sketch – some six feet tall, with a huge and rotund belly that started under his chin and finished at his knees. He had a peculiar habit of lifting up his head and staring at the sky when he spoke. 'Good day, Mrs Jolly,' he said, addressing a passing cloud. 'I'm Gabriel Everest . . . used to do business with the former proprietor. Now, I'm given to understand that Pops Barber-shop will soon be open for business?' Before I could explain the situation to his chin, he went on, 'We have some new and exciting lines you might be interested in . . . let me show you.' He opened his case. I tried to tell him how the world and his wife were doing everything possible to prevent me from opening the barber's shop, but he was adamant. 'I'll be back to take your order in a couple of weeks.' Bidding good day to the chimney, he took his leave.

'Good God, what's all this?' Maggie helped me to carry the samples in from the pavement. What on earth were we going to do with six bottles of Heavenly shampoo, nine squirters of Eiderdown lather, three bright purple sachets of Sprout hair-restorer, and a motley selection of condoms? Closer scrutiny revealed four packets of extra-sensitive, two boxes of erotica, six packages of short and scarlet, and a huge helping of pink extra-long (with or without teats).

'Bloody 'ell!' chuckled Sonya, when I showed them to her. 'Gi' the buggers ter me. I'll find a use fer 'em!'

I refused. 'I shall wait for this Gabriel Everest to come back and take the bally lot away!'

Sonya pointed out that they were samples, and samples needed to be tried and tested. 'No, Sonya,' I said. I had a dreadful vision of Sonya standing on my doorstep, reporting to Gabriel Everest in the loudest and most graphic manner every gory detail regarding performance, durability, sensitivity and value for money. The thought terrified me.

Saturday, August 29th

Maggie's frantically digging her bolt-hole and Tom says if I try and get him in school before he's five he'll run away. I told him I intended to do just that. Unfortunately he hasn't run away – he's just gone into a sulk. Wilhelmina's joined him.

I had a pleasant surprise, though. Fred and Bertha Twistle came to see me. Bertha said they'd had a talk and that Fred wanted to tell me something. Fred said he was sorry for the way he'd shouted at me. 'The landlady at the Stag thinks I look butch wi' me new 'aircut . . . so I'm not wearin' me cap no more!'

We're friends again. What's more, half the regulars from the Stag are queuing up for appointments. It's an ill wind, they say. Which reminds me – I must try and find out whether Larkin's discovered the bald patch yet.

Sunday, August 30th

The man from the builders tells me it would be cheaper to pull the house down than to put right what's wrong with it, particularly the collapsed floor in the parlour.

I think old Pops is getting impatient. He keeps leaving subtle hints, like writing 'Sod yer all!' across the front window in shaving-cream.

I actually earned four pounds today! Two short back and sides, a shampoo and a poodle trim, only it wasn't a poodle. It was a bulldog. Four-legged animals are off my list. It's a wonder I escaped with all my fingers intact.

Monday, August 31st

I had a letter from Tiffany today. It was six pages long and full of woe. 'How are we expected to live next door to people who actually wash their car?' she asks. 'And the man hasn't made one pass at me. Would you believe they have been seen to kiss each other at the door in the morning? A man kissing his own wife! My dear . . . I despair!' (So do I. Whatever would she think of Casey's Court?)

Barny Singleton sent me a note via his son. It said that if I was prepared to give up the notion of ever re-opening the barber-shop, he would enlist the help of a couple of his mates to repair the shop-floor. What did I say?

I sent a reply outlining my plans to go ahead and get permission to start business as soon as possible. Furthermore, I intended to make it the best barber-shop in the whole of Lancashire. Then I sat down and wrote a long letter to the Council.

Tuesday, September 1st

I think Maggie's cracking up. She's become fanatical about that hole in the back yard. I caught her lowering provisions into it, together with her precious tin hat. 'The buggers won't get me without a fight!' she said, flinging a clod of earth at Lucky when he cocked his leg over her spade.

Sonya's got the most magnificent black eye. When I asked her how she got it, she wouldn't go into details except to say that the fellow was well endowed and 'I should 'a known better than to sneak up be'ind 'im on all fours'. The mind boggles.

I actually washed and set Larkin's hair, and I'm glad to say that the glue held tight.

Wednesday, September 2nd

Had an urgent phone-call from Tiffany. She was excited because the police had come to her door. 'They were looking for that crazy woman,' she said. 'They seem to think she might be hiding out in one of the sheds or garages hereabouts – or even have dug a hole, which apparently is one of her weaknesses. We've all been told to stay on the alert, because she was last seen in this vicinity!' I told her to calm down. No one would dare to dig a hole in Tiffany's beautifully manicured lawn.

I related the tale to Maggie. We both had a good laugh about it.

Thursday, September 3rd

There are two daisies coming up from the hole in the front parlour – they're really quite pretty.

Granny Grabber caught hold of Tom as he was passing her house. It seems she's had a word with Bertha Twistle, and is ready to have her perm. 'She grabbed my arse!' Tom complained. I was not putting up with that kind of language, so I spanked the offending article and put it to bed. 'It's not fair!' he protested. 'Sonya Pitts can say it, so why can't I?' I must have another talk with Sonya.

When I went round to Granny Grabber's she grabbed mine too, as I arrived, and again as I was leaving. No wonder the milkman calls twice a day. Her perm turned out all right, though – a bit wild perhaps, but she didn't complain. She's a wicked little thing – rather like an elf, with small pointed ears and bright brown eyes. She wears long slippers which flap when she walks, and her parlour is like Aladdin's cave, all brass and shiny things, with the

75

delicious smell of fresh-baked bread permeating the air. She has a mangy-looking dog called Skidaddle, who seems harassed and terribly nervous. Skidaddle keeps his distance, perched on top of the dresser, ever alert and trembling. He only came down once while I was there, for a quick gulp of water. That was a fatal mistake. The poor thing's completely bald on his rear end.

Friday, September 4th

Maggie woke me up in the night. 'There's somebody trying to get in the front door,' she said, in a whisper loud enough to scare even me. 'D'you reckon it's that Mad Aggie?'

I didn't reckon anything, and I wasn't going down to peer through the letter-box – not after what happened last time. I crept to the window and tried to sneak a look from the corner of the curtains, while Maggie stood by with her half-filled receptacle from beneath the bed. I couldn't see a thing; all the street-lights were out, and I daren't open the window. There was only one thing to do. Maggie and I sat on the floor with our backs to the door, and there we stayed till morning light, clinging to each other for dear life. Whoever it was didn't give up easily, because the sounds went on for ages.

At first sign of daylight, when the intruder appeared to have given up, I raced down and called the police. A constable was out in no time – a nice enough fellow, with heaps of advice. He was quick to assure us that crime in Casey's Court was virtually unknown. 'You're not down south now, missus,' he said, obviously proud of the fact that the last time he made an arrest was when some unfortunate fellow sneezed so hard at the local dog-track that he caused the whippets to make a false start. 'A quiet life is what we're used to in these parts.' He looked stern. 'I understand there's been more pandemonium in Casey's Court since you arrived than ever before.'

Before he sauntered off, he advised us to have a phone extension put in upstairs. 'But don't you be calling the station every time your imagination runs riot!' Then he looked me up and down, clicking his tongue in disapproval. 'There's a story going round the station,' he said accusingly, 'that one of the local Council officials told the superintendent that we ought to keep an eye on this house.'

'Well there you are then!' At least one person thought we might be in danger. 'He must have heard there was a dangerous criminal on the loose!'

The constable clicked a good deal louder. 'Oh aye! He did think that. He said as how he came to this door in all good faith, to do his bounden duty. And a young redhead answered his knock . . . pissed as a newt! It also seems he was offered a cup of gin, to lure him inside. Now I have to tell you, Mrs Jolly, we're respectable law-abiding folk here. And I'll thank you not to start down a road that can only lead to degradation and corruption. That's all. Good day to you.'

Maggie was furious. 'Silly old bugger!' she said. 'The fellow lives in a dream world.'

I was in total agreement. We had a pair of marathon bonkers on one side of us, an afflicted hypochondriac on the other, a granny who wasn't particular what she grabbed as long as it was warm and squashy, and a seedy – if loveable – 'provider' who indulged in throwing dollops of ice-cream at men's naked danglers. On top of everything, we were plagued by a cantankerous old ghost and some desperate criminal who had already made two attempts to break into our house. And what about Grandad Pitts running riot with his air-rifle? If you ask me, Casey's Court is a hotbed of vice and corruption. (But I love it! I'm even picking up the language.)

Saturday, September 5th

We spent a quiet day today. I did a mountainous pile of ironing. After dinner, Maggie played snap with the children till they caught her cheating. In the face of their united accusations she ran off in a sulk. She didn't emerge from her dug-out till four o'clock, when Tom pelted her with his tiddly-winks.

Wilhelmina watched me like a hawk as I was getting her clothes ready for school on Monday. 'I'm not going!' she declared, folding her arms and pouting.

'We'll see about that, young madam!' I said. The argument raged on until Lucky cocked his leg over her snap cards.

Roll on Monday. Let the poor teacher cope with her.

Sunday, September 6th

Went for a walk in the park. Tom disturbed a wasp-nest, and we all got stung. Tom got a smack when he shouted at the top of his voice, 'Lucky's got swollen cobblers!'

Monday, September 7th

I was drawing my bedroom curtains last night when I caught sight of Barny Singleton. He was escorting the same gorgeous brunette to her car. He glimpsed me at the window, and straightway put his arm round her and kissed her in the most intimate manner. I shut the curtains quickly, not wanting him to have the pleasure of thinking he was making me jealous. I couldn't get him out of my mind, though. And, when I fell asleep, I dreamed it was me he was holding in that close, wonderful embrace. (Am I falling in love, I ask myself?)

Later in the day, I had a phone-call from Tiffany. She was in a terrible state. 'I think Justin's having an affair with that bitch next door!' she sobbed. (That cured me of Barny Singleton. Men! They're all the same.)

I'm afraid Wilhelmina's getting out of control. At ten thirty this morning, just when I was congratulating myself on having safely deposited her at school, the phone rang. It was the headmistress, Mrs Hepher (pronounced Hee-fur). The conversation went something like this:

'Is that Mrs Jolly?'

'Yes.'

'Mrs Jolly, this is Mrs Hepher, and I'm afraid I must insist that you come to school immediately!'

'Really? Why's that, Mrs Hepher?' (I hated school more than Wilhelmina did.)

'It's your daughter, Wilhelmina. I'm sorry to say she has proved herself to be a very bad influence on the other children. She's rude, arrogant, aggressive and extremely spiteful!' (Fancy Mrs Hepher not noticing Wilhelmina's *good* qualities.)

'Oh, Mrs Hepher! Surely she can't have made such a

bad impression in such a short time? She's only been there an hour and a half.'

I would have gone into great detail about the good qualities in Wilhelmina's personality, but when I broached the subject Mrs Hepher cut me short by demanding in a no-nonsense voice, '*What* good qualities?' She had me stumped. 'Come and fetch her at once! We will not tolerate hooliganism in this school!'

All the way, I wondered what on earth madam had been doing to upset Mrs Hepher. Half an hour later, I had the beast in tow and was marching her back home. She was silent, and I was furious! In the space of ninety minutes this obnoxious and deceivingly pretty little girl had caused chaos and uproar, seemingly without the slightest regret. I couldn't believe it when Mrs Hepher outlined the devastating catalogue of events. 'It started in the playground, when the children were lining up to go in,' she reported. 'It seems your daughter' (I do wish she wouldn't keep calling her that) 'thought fit to stuff a long hairy caterpillar down the trousers of the boy in front of her. Well! Of course, there was absolute chaos . . . six lines of impressionable and frightened children, panicked by the boy's screams, all fleeing in different directions. I tell you, Mrs Jolly, I have never seen anything quite like it. And I hope I never have the misfortune to see anything like it again. We found two children trembling in the rubbish bins, and another group had climbed the cherry tree and would not be enticed down! Several more were swinging from the sweet-pea supports in our nature garden, having trampled all our hard work underfoot. And at least four had run home to tell their parents the school was on fire. I can assure you, Mrs Jolly, it was a devastating experience. To cap it all, the oldest member of our teaching staff . . . Mr Plumm . . . was so affected by the panic that he dived fully clothed into the swimming pool. Needless to say he has applied for early retirement.'

It was naïve of me to think that was the full extent of madam's escapade!

'No sooner had we all recovered from that ordeal than your daughter's class teacher burst into my office with another creation of Wilhelmina Jolly's fertile imagination. It seems the art lesson had been well under way when Miss Clutterbuck noticed the absence of your daughter and another somewhat timid little creaturē. It was this child who was brought before me by the harassed Miss Clutterbuck. My dear Mrs Jolly, there are no words with which I can effectively convey to you the terrifying appearance of this poor little mite. I can only point out that the entire year's stock of paint was used up in the space of twenty minutes . . . not to mention the goose-feathers brought in for our pantomime.'

I was duly horrified. But if I thought that was the end of it, I was fooling myself. 'The final straw came, Mrs Jolly, during our main assembly . . . a time when the whole school congregates for a period of quiet and reflective thought . . . a time when we offer our thanks to the Lord, and joyfully sing his praises. Your daughter, I am sorry to say, threw the entire gathering into pandemonium. And to make matters worse, Mrs Jolly, we were entertaining a most eminent and distinguished visitor, the Reverend Siniter, a most sober and pious servant of the Lord.'

I wondered what madam had done to throw an entire school assembly 'into pandemonium', but I soon found out. Mrs Hepher is a woman who 'believes in giving every child the opportunity to redeem itself'. Once Wilhelmina had been seen to apologize to the painted one, she was allowed the privilege of helping the prefects wheel the piano from the music room to the assembly hall, and given a place on the stage to sing with the choir. 'We were deep into the first hymn . . . "Oh, what heroes thou hast bred" . . . when poor Mrs Hardly appeared to be experiencing some small difficulty in playing the piano. I, of course, tried to draw attention from her curious predicament by raising my voice and leading the school in an uplifting chorus.' According to Mrs Hepher's account of what followed, it seems that the singing increased in volume until the swell of voices became quite deafening, resulting in some of the younger infants being completely overcome and reduced to tears. All the while, Mrs Hardly, in the finest tradition of showbusiness, bravely carried on – even though the piano continued to move away from her at an alarming rate. 'That poor woman is on the point of a nervous breakdown.' Apparently the piano inched its way across the stage until Mrs Hardly's arms were fully outstretched, and she was hanging on to her stool by the skin of her cheeks. It was at this point that the maestro fell prostrate before the whole assembly, which (apart from the more adult members, who gasped in horror) collapsed in fits of hysterical laughter.

'Of course the culprit was found to be Wilhelmina. She had abused the privilege of wheeling the piano into assembly by tying a skipping-rope around the piano-leg, and pulling it towards her the moment Mrs Hardly began playing.'

Well, it certainly seems that madam was more ingenious than I was at school, I thought with sneaking admiration, which grew considerably when Mrs Hepher went on to explain that Wilhelmina had been banished from the stage and placed in the front row of the baby class 'to shame her before the rest of the school'. Order was eventually restored, with every child lined up in smart straight rows.

Mrs Hardly had retired to the rest-room in a nervous condition, and the Reverend Siniter kindly took over the duties of piano-player. It was when he struck up the first notes of 'All things bright and beautiful' that Wilhelmina decided to liven things up. Mrs Hepher still hadn't recovered. 'When Wilhelmina fell backwards in a pretend faint the whole of 4c and half of 3a toppled over, one after the other, like a pack of dominoes!'

I didn't wait to hear any more, but expressed my gratitude that at least Mrs Hepher had not expelled her. 'Make no mistake,' she warned, 'if she has not seen fit to mend her ways after a week's suspension, I will have no hesitation in closing our doors to her altogether.'

I've spoken to a solicitor, who thinks I should be allowed to carry on Pops's barber-shop. He's writing to the planning official.

Tuesday, September 8th

There's word going round that there's been another meeting at the Council offices, but no one's heard anything officially. 'I rang the buggers up,' Sonya told me. 'It's our future yer discussin', I told 'em; we've a right ter know what's goin' on!' She's not one for mincing words, isn't our Sonya, which the Council soon found out when they told her that no firm decision had been made. When it was, she, like everyone else down Casey's Court, would be informed. 'Yer buggers!' she retaliated. 'Yer all think yer a cut above us. But I'll tell yer this! Just you sods come round 'ere wi' eviction notices, an' yer'll gerrem stuffed that far up yer arses yer'll think yer breakfast is stuck in yer bloody throats!'

'Good Lord, Sonya . . . you mustn't talk to people like

that.' I despair of her, I really do. 'What did the fellow say?'

'Slammed the soddin' phone down, di'n't 'e? Got no manners whatsoever!'

Wilhelmina's confined to her bedroom. 'It doesn't bother me!' she said. It doesn't bother me either.

My black eyebrow pencil went missing. I thought Maggie might have borrowed it, but she was most offended when I asked her. 'What would I want with that?' she retorted. 'You don't need such frivolous items in a bunker!' I found it under the scullery-table, clutched in Tom's fat little hand. He'd used it to draw a face on his thing. Lucky was under the table with him, and threatened violence when I tried to get him out. So I put two slices of bread in the toaster, and he was up and out like a shot.

Sonya minded the children while Maggie and I tried to tidy the floor in the barber-shop. We took up all the jagged bits and went to the local tip to see if we could find some planks. There were four gypsyish women down there foraging about for bits they could use or sell. They thought Maggie and I were trespassing on their patch, and they picked a fight with us. We had no intention of being bullied, though, and we gave as good as we got. As luck would have it, we were close to where a market trader had dumped a load of rotten fruit and veg. Those gypsies didn't know what had hit them! There were no holds barred, and within minutes the blighters had taken to their heels.

On the way home we got some funny looks. I suppose we did look something of a spectacle, all tattered and torn and dragging two great planks behind us. There must have been upward of twenty dogs following our scent. When we paused for breath outside the fishmonger's he rushed out and offered us a pound each to keep going. When we got home Sonya wouldn't let us in. She poked her nose through the letter-box, shouting, 'Sod off! Yer stink to 'igh 'eaven!'

'You let me in, Sonya Pitts!' I said, painfully conscious of the two faces leering at me from the bedroom window. When she remained adamant, I marched Maggie round to the back yard. 'This is my house,' I shouted from the middle of the flagstones, 'and I will not be locked out!' Whereupon the door was flung open and a bucket of water sloshed over us both.

'Yer ain't bloody well comin' in 'ere stinkin' like polecats!' called Sonya. Since we were already soaked to the skin, we put up little resistance when Sonya refilled her bucket from the outside tap and came at us like a tidal wave. 'Yer can come in now,' she said, standing at the door with two towels. And, like two little lambs, we squelched in. 'I expect yer think I'm a right cow?' she ventured. The thought had never crossed my mind!

Wednesday, September 9th

I earned twelve pounds today – the best yet. I cut a little lad's hair from across the way – he was really pleased when I declined to use the pudding-basin his mother brought. I washed and set little Larkin's hair. The glue's holding well. Then there was a head-shave for Fred Twistle, a trim for Bertha, and a curly perm for one of Sonya's clients, by the name of Marmaduke.

I was amazed when I went into Sonya's back parlour to perm Marmaduke's hair. Grandad Pitts had gone into town to collect his pension, leaving behind pathetic barricades which Sonya lifted out of the way with one hand.

That parlour was a revelation! Second-hand books were piled high against one wall, reaching to the ceiling. There were wooden chests lined up on either side of the fireplace, so stuffed full of old rags that they resembled twin mountains. Multitudes of shoes lined the floor and there wasn't a chair that didn't have a garment slung over it. There were two lovely little landscape paintings on the wall over the fireplace – both hanging at a sixty-degree angle. And decorating the tiled hearth was what appeared to be a whole dinner-service, complete with gravy stains, dried tea leaves, fish bones and orange pips. Hanging from the brass pole above the window were two curtains of indistinguishable colour, one perfectly draped, the other in tatters. 'The bloody cat from next door's responsible fer that!' explained Sonya. 'The silly sod snuk in 'ere, then threw a panic 'cause it couldn't gerrout!'

I did my best to hide the amazement I felt when first seeing that parlour. But Sonya twigged my reaction in the very first instant. 'Yer shocked, ain't yer?' she asked, waving her arms about and kicking out her leg to make a space for Marmaduke's chair.

'No!' I fibbed.

'Yer bloody liar!' she roared, bursting into laughter and shaking her peroxide head at me. 'Everybody's shocked when they come in 'ere. But I don't gi' a tinker's cuss. I'm a slag . . . I am, an' I don't care a bugger who knows it.' That's what I like about Sonya. She's straightforward.

Thursday, September 10th

Maggie and I worked like Trojans today. We cut the jagged bits back from the hole in the parlour floor. Then we carefully measured up and sawed the two great planks we'd dragged from the tip. That done, we carried the pieces in, one at a time, and hammered them to the joists until the best part of the hole was covered over. It was a pity the hammering caused all the plaster to fall off the walls. We looked like snowmen when we'd finished. Another curious thing was the way the noise next door increased. The more we banged away, the more they did. It was nerve-racking. 'I expect they think it's a bonking competition,' piped up Wilhelmina. I was shocked! Where does she get these ideas from? I wonder if that freckle-faced Winnie is as wide-eyed and innocent as she looks.

'It's just echoes,' Maggie told her, trying to divert her attention from what went on next door.

'It's not,' came the retort, 'those two are bonking. They're *always* bonking.'

I charged forward, with the intention of accompanying madam back to her room, but I fell straight down the hole instead. Maggie shot forward to help me, somehow lost her footing, and ended up sitting in the barber's chair, which swivelled round at such alarming speed that her false teeth took flight through the open window, and impaled themselves on the barber's pole outside. 'Guggy 'ell!' she exclaimed, when I finally brought the chair to a standstill. It had gone round at such a rate that I really wondered whether old Pops might have helped it along.

The performance of retrieving Maggie's teeth was a nightmare. Suffice it to say it was a toss-up who'd get to them first – me or the rag-a-bone man's horse. (I think an early night for all is called for.)

Friday, September 11th

The barber's parlour is beginning to look ship-shape again. There's only a little hole showing now, about a foot square. But we've positioned one of the chairs over it, and no one would ever know. We've stuck posters over the patches on the wall where the plaster fell off.

Maggie seems fully recovered, thank goodness. And Grandad Pitts came knocking on the door today. 'What sort of 'aircuts d'yer do?' he said, his gun slung under his arm and his flat cap squashed further over his ears than ever.

'Haircuts?' I was curious, because under that cap he was as bald as a billiard ball. 'Well, a trim . . . or a short back and sides. Is it for a friend?'

'Naw! Look 'ere . . .' he seemed unusually embarrassed '. . . d'yer do owt different? I mean . . . can yer restore 'air, when it's gone?' When I explained how impossible that was he brandished his gun at me and stormed off, calling back, 'Yer no bloody good! Any silly fool can chop 'air *off*! It teks a better man ter put it back!'

When I mentioned it to Sonya later on, she laughed and told me to 'tek no notice o' the ol' fool'. She seemed to think he's taken a fancy to some woman. 'Gone all moony-eyed an' broody,' she said. 'Can't think why 'e's so bloody concerned about *that* end. It's the *other* end 'as needs some'at putting back!' She can be cruel.

I had another male visitor, about nine thirty this evening. It was Barny Singleton. Maggie had gone to bed, and I was reckoning up what money we had left. When the rates are paid, there'll be about eight hundred pounds left in the building society. It's enough to keep us going for about three months, but I'll need to get something organized long before then. I really enjoy this barbering lark, and it's beginning to earn us a few pounds now, so I hope that solicitor can get it all sorted out.

When the knock came at the door I wondered who it could be at such a late hour, not having forgotten the business of the green-eyed monster. When, on my insistence, he identified himself, I opened the door, my hackles already up for a fight. I don't know whether it was the soft glow of the street light silhouetting his tall, powerful physique, or whether it was the light from the passage which bathed his dark handsome features, or whether, even, it was the way he brought those gloriously dark and tantalizing eyes to bear on me, but my hackles fell, my knees went to mush, and my heart beat so fast that I was afraid he must hear it.

'Hello, Jessica,' he murmured in that strong velvety voice. 'I'm sorry it's so late, but I do want to talk with you.' He inclined his head, stretched his gaze beyond me to the parlour, and asked softly, 'Will you invite me in?' How could I refuse?

Once inside the parlour, and seated in the high-backed chair in front of the fireplace, Barny Singleton waited patiently while I made him a cup of tea. On my return, he took the tea and politely thanked me, waiting until I was seated opposite him before broaching the reason for his visit. Casey's Court is one of those wonderful places where you can't sneeze without somebody four doors away offering you a handkerchief. 'I know your every move, Jessica,' he said with a fantastic crooked smile. 'I know that your parlour floor collapsed, and that you've been clever enough to repair it . . . even if you did bring the powerful atmosphere of the tip back with you.' He laughed, his dark caressing eyes never once leaving my face. When I would have defended my adventure as being one of necessity, he put his hand up to stay me. 'No,

Jessica. Hear me out . . . then you can have your say. I'm not belittling your attempt to make a success here, believe me. On the contrary, I admire the way you've stuck to your principles, and, from what I'm told – together with the fact that I've already lost two of my regular customers to you – you're not doing a bad job at barbering either.' When I assured him that I intended to do even better, and that my determination to re-open Pops's parlour was as strong as ever, he said, 'I can see you're a woman of character. The sort of woman I want.' Good grief! I began trembling with excitement – was he about to propose? 'You're attractive, smart, well-spoken . . . and you appear to have a natural flair for hairdressing.' He obviously didn't know about Larkin's glued-on patch. 'I've been looking for someone like you for some time.' He leaned forward to rest his hand on mine. How I didn't leap up through the ceiling I will never know. Then, with his warm strong fingers sending thrills down my spine, and his soft voice making love to me, he put the question. 'Jessica . . . will you come and work for me?'

The magic was broken. 'How dare you?' I snatched my hand away and leapt to my feet. 'You know you can't stop me . . . so you try and get me to join forces with you. Just like the big companies who can't face up to competition, so either force it out of business or buy it out.' He'd do neither as far as I was concerned.

'I'm sorry you feel that way, Jessica,' he said, rising to leave. 'I didn't mean it as an insult or as a way of curbing your enthusiasm. I'd just rather you used that energy and enthusiasm on my behalf. I'll pay you good wages, and you can work the hours which suit you.'

'Oh, I *will*! I'll work here, in my own shop. And, as I told you once before, Barny Singleton, I'll build my business up until I become a *real* menace. We don't think alike, you and I, because I feel there's enough room for all of us, whereas you, and people like you, want it all for themselves. Well, tough! Because I'll not be shifted from my own little dream . . . you can count on that!'

For a long tense moment we stood facing each other, his dark eyes burning into mine, and I could feel myself melting beneath that passionate gaze. Without warning, he reached out and grabbed me by the shoulders, pulling me to him and kissing me full and long on the mouth. When he just as swiftly thrust me from him and turned to storm out of the house, I was left trembling from head to foot. My mouth was tingling and every sense in my body was screaming out for him to come back and take me in his arms again. 'Oh, Barny,' I murmured, 'why did we have to start out as enemies?' The only answer I received was a slight rush of cold air past my face, a curious whistling sound, and the front door crashing shut. 'It's all right for you, Pops! I'm only a woman, and I need loving . . . you're past all that.' When I returned to the parlour, there wasn't a chair left standing. 'Sorry, Pops,' I said. I must have hurt his feelings.

Saturday, September 12th

We all went down the market today. What an adventure! Maggie got called 'that young lady' by the butcher. Tom found a 50p coin, and Wilhelmina won a lucky dip. I bought some fresh haddock for tea, a pair of new household slippers (the left one got mangled down the hole in the parlour) and a lovely lemon top with a plunging neckline. I'll save that for when I'm cleaning the upstairs windows, in case Barny's watching. Lucky wasn't forgotten, either. We bought him a bag of chews. I told him they weren't for eating now, but he sang so prettily for one that I hadn't the heart to refuse. We all sat by the knicker-stall eating ice-creams while he ate his chew-stick. Afterwards, both he and Tom were sick.

When we'd finished our shopping, whom should we bump into but Grandad Pitts. And my word, wasn't he spruced up – with a new chequered flat cap, a clean white tie and polished shoes, and a grin on his face to ward off evil. ''Ello, Maggie Flaherty,' he said to Maggie, who, I was astonished to see, was blushing furiously.

'Oh, hello, Ethelbert,' she replied, catching Wilhelmina a sharp cuff round the ear when she began to giggle. Tom was too busy sticking his nose up Ethelbert's gun barrel to follow the proceedings.

After that, it was one thing after another. First of all Lucky wriggled out of his collar and set off in pursuit of an enormous Great Dane. Then we had to rush Tom, his nose, and Ethelbert's gun barrel to hospital, where the ensuing operation was accompanied by much screaming and panic. And when Wilhelmina was run down by a geriatric hooligan in a wheelchair, she set up such a wail that we were all asked to leave. It was most embarrassing.

Once outside, with the doors firmly closed behind us, Maggie shyly accepted Ethelbert's offer of a cup of tea. They skipped off like young lovers, one as bald as a coot beneath his flat cap, and the other with false teeth that could take to the air at any minute.

By the time I got home (minus Lucky, and having lost Maggie to the arms of Ethelbert) I was well and truly shattered. Throwing down the three loaded shopping bags in the passage, I left the monsters to their fighting, got myself a welcome cup of tea, and put my feet up. It was lovely. (Not so lovely later, though, when I found all four of Bertha Twistle's cats finishing off the haddock.)

Tiffany rang today, in a state. 'He *is* cavorting with that shameless hussy next door,' she cried, 'and it's all your fault, Jessica Jolly! If you hadn't moved out, she wouldn't have been able to move in.' I asked her what she was going to do about it. 'Kill myself, of course!' I swiftly reminded her that she'd always promised me that lovely red hat of hers. But then I asked myself what I would do with a red hat in Casey's Court. Only the other day, I'd heard a woman in the corner shop say, 'You can allus depend on it. A red hat on top means no bloomers underneath.' So I asked Tiffany what she intended to do with that frog-on-a-toadstool in her garden. 'You're heartless!' she moaned, and slammed the phone down. She does have a tendency to over-dramatize. I'm sure she'll ring back.

I've been reading about Edwina Currie. What a misinformed lady she is. (There are some round here who wouldn't describe her as a lady. The woman in the tripe shop was quite put out. 'Silly pratt! I've raised seven children on meat 'n' tatty pies an' mushy peas . . . an' there ain't a one as couldn't swing that silly bugger over their shoulders! Tall an' strong are my children, all on 'em!' She's right. One is a policeman, two have their own rag-a-bone business, two work as bouncers in a seedy club in town (that's the two girls) and the youngest two, aged six and ten, have just started a window-cleaning round. (Edwina's friend, Maggie, should take note of such enterprise.)

Also, she had something to say about the Government's other idea – a national lottery to help fund the NHS. 'What! Yer mean they give yer all a number, and put 'em in a hat? Yer really mean ter say I've to wait fer my number to come up afore I can have my bunions done? I've never heard owt like it in all my life!' Neither have I.

Monday, September 14th

I rang the school today. 'Will it be in order for me to bring Wilhelmina in tomorrow, Mrs Hepher?' I asked.

'No! It will not!' she retorted. 'You may bring her in on Friday!' I expect she wants the weekend to get over it.

'What am I going to do with myself till Friday?' wailed madam. I told her. She wasn't too partial to the list of twenty jobs I suggested. 'I'd rather not, thank you,' she said. 'I'll play with Winnie, 'cause she's not going to school either.' She wasn't very pleased when the truant officer tracked Winnie to Maggie's bunker, where Wilhelmina and Winnie were playing soldiers. When the man marched her protesting friend off to school, Wilhelmina threw a fit and wouldn't come out of the hole. It caused a great uproar, ending up with Maggie throwing clods of earth at her. 'Get out!' she yelled, growing more panic-stricken by the minute. 'That's *my* bolt-hole . . . and you're trespassing!'

Such was the furore that Lucky hid in the lavvy. An alien voice shouted from the upstairs window next door, 'We're on nights here! Would you mind being quiet?' (and then the house began rocking again). And little Larkin, who'd been in the garden hanging out her washing, gave a little scream and fled to the safety of her parlour, leaving a combustion trail behind her as if she was jet-propelled. Tom took up forces with Wilhelmina until a clod of earth caught him on the ear, at which point he began leathering Wilhelmina. Maggie declared herself to be the victor, and peace was restored.

I don't feel well.

Tuesday, September 15th

Maggie was up at the crack of dawn this morning. She gave her teeth a double dose of bleach (she must be the only person who's got snow-white gums) and then she spent a full hour trying on first one dress, then another. That done, she commandeered the scullery for a strip-out wash, and I was bullied into washing and setting her hair, even before I'd had my customary fight with the toaster. Then she dug out a pair of high-heeled shoes from her chest. Honestly! It was plain to see they were crippling her. She looked like a ballet-dancer going on tiptoe through a mine-field. Next came the powder and lipstick – you'd have thought it had been laid on with a brickie's trowel. The eyebrows were the worst, though. 'I never have liked the flat shape of my brows,' she said, squinting in the mirror, and promptly shaved off her old ones and drew two brand new ones on her forehead. (I have to give the children their due – they didn't laugh when she turned round. They just looked astonished – as did the terrified Lucky – and then all three fled.)

The reason for all this pruning was made evident at ten o'clock, when Grandad Pitts presented himself at the door, looking like a recycled window dummy. 'I won't be back till late,' called Maggie (lipstick all over her teeth), 'so don't wait up.' I watched the two of them totter up Casey's Court – he with his trousers flapping in the breeze, she with legs that kept collapsing outwards when her heels went over. I'm convinced she'll come crawling home with both ankles broken. When they'd turned the corner, I went back inside, feeling really lonely.

Not for long, though. Ten minutes later Sonya was round, bearing gifts in the form of half a slightly mangled lemon meringue. 'Oh, what a lovely thought,' I said, pleased to have her company. 'I'll make us a cup of tea to go with it.'

'Shame ter waste it,' she said. 'I scooped up the best bits after 'e'd gone . . . it were 'ardly spoiled.'

'After who'd gone?' I asked, thinking she probably meant Grandad Pitts.

'That feller I told yer about,' she replied, 'yer know! The one as liked 'is danglers plastered. Only 'e's gone orf ice-cream, an' tekken a fancy ter lemon meringue.'

I had a cheese cracker, while Sonya wolfed down every last bit of that mangled meringue.

I did four haircuts today, a beard trim, and two sets. The phone's ringing more and more, and I can really see myself beginning to earn a proper living at it soon! But there's still no news from the solicitor about opening the shop.

Wednesday, September 16th

A man came to the door today. He was quite a formidable sight. He must have been seven feet tall, with piercing dark eyes, a straggly ginger beard, and a great swell of a middle. 'Are you supporting our cause?' he asked, thrusting his stomach into the passage and playing with his beard.

'What cause is that?' I didn't like the look of the fellow at all.

'Why . . . Casey's Court!' he exploded, his little eyes

popping open. 'The *preservation* of Casey's Court!' As he leaned forward, I suddenly caught a whiff of him. Phew! Maggie and I coming back from the tip must have been like a breath of spring compared to him. I had to cling to the door for support. 'My name is Ben,' he said, with some pride, 'Ben Kelly.' I twigged! He must be the 'Smelly Kelly' Sonya told me about. Squashing a leaflet into my hand, he urged, 'You take that, m'dear! And you read it from end to end. Because when the time comes – when we're called to account for ourselves – every man, woman and child will be expected to do their duty!' (My God! He's as fanatical as Grandad Pitts!)

After he'd departed, I rushed about opening doors and windows to let a through breeze drive away the lingering aroma. It smelt as if a herd of billy goats had been driven through.

When I told Sonya about it, she bent double laughing. 'One o' these days, gal,' she roared, 'us women'll get together an' 'e won't know what's 'it 'im!'

'What do you mean?' I asked nervously.

'I means what I says! All the women i' Casey's Court 'ave long been sayin' as 'ow we should pounce on Smelly Kelly, strip the bugger off, an' gi' 'im a bath 'e'd not forget in 'undred years!' She seemed to relish the prospect; the thought of it terrified me.

'You can count me out,' I told her.

'I bloody won't,' she roared. 'Yer one o' the Casey Court women now, Jessica Jolly! An' if the vote's tekken ter do the deed, then yer'll 'ave no choice in the matter!' When she saw how horrified I was, she added, 'Don't worry . . . I'll see yer don't get landed wi' the scrag-end.' I suppose I must be grateful for small mercies.

Sonya reckons Grandad Pitts 'is right gone on that mam-in-law o' yourn'. Well, I know she's smitten with him, and that's a fact. As my dear mother used to say, I hope it doesn't end in tears.

Tiffany must be sulking, because she never rang back. I began to think I might have been a bit insensitive to her problem, so I phoned her. The first time there was no reply. The second time she slammed the phone down on me. And the third time, I recognized her husband's voice. All I said was 'Hello' and he began whispering things like 'Darling, I've asked you not to ring me here . . . we must be careful . . .' When I tried to interrupt, he murmured in a suggestive voice, 'I know you want me, angel. Oh, and I want you! If only you knew how I long to take off your clothes one by one . . . to stroke every inch of your smooth skin, and to wash it with my tongue. Oh, my angel . . . I can't wait till we're together again . . . alone, just the two of us. Ssh! Don't speak . . . you don't know what your voice does to me. Wait till tomorrow night, my delicious darling. Till then, I'll hold the memory of you close in my heart. Oh, how I yearn for you! How I need your velvet naked skin next to mine. We must be patient. Till tomorrow . . .' I stood there with the phone still in my hand for some long moments afterwards. I was shocked! I was jealous! And I found myself day-dreaming about Barny Singleton. Then I remembered Tiffany, and I felt ashamed. Poor Tiffany, I thought. How on earth would she cope with it all? I'll ring later, at a time when she's more likely to be in.

Thursday, September 17th

Hip, hip, hooray! The planning people have backed down! It seems old Pops never officially notified anyone that he had ceased trading, so to all intents and purposes it's still a barber-shop. There are a few official forms to be dealt with, and the registering of it in my name. But nothing to worry about. 'Yer'll do more business now, gal!' cheered Sonya. 'Not everybody likes 'avin' their 'air cut in their own front parlour.' I do hope she's right.

I was so thrilled that at long last I was going to open the barber-shop and have proper customers that when the representative phoned and asked whether I would now like to place an order I just agreed with everything he suggested. It was only later that I realized I couldn't remember what I'd ordered. I must not be so foolhardy, if I'm to be a successful businesswoman. Maggie and I dusted the barber's parlour. Then, while I put a pile of clean towels on the shelf and lined up all my bits and pieces on the worktop between the basins, she hung a brand new placard in the window, telling the world that 'Jolly's Hair Salon' would be open for business from 9 A.M. Friday morning. It felt really good to see my name up in lights. Also, I rather thought that 'Hair Salon' was much more fashionable than 'Pops Barber-shop'.

Unfortunately, old Pops didn't feel the same way. Just before bedtime, Maggie and I heard an uproar coming from the front parlour. When we crept in, it was to see both barber-chairs sucked up to the ceiling, and every last artefact – shampoo bottles, hairspray canisters, hair-brushes and towels – whizzing round the room at fright-ening speed. The window blind was viciously rolling and unrolling, and both basins were overflowing where the taps had been left on at full pelt. When Maggie opened her mouth to give old Pops a piece of her mind, she was lifted bodily from the floor and suspended, her dangling legs kicking out and a look of sheer terror on her face.

'You old bugger, Pops!' I yelled above the din, shaking my fist. 'Stop it at once!' I tried appealing to his business acumen, but there was no consoling him. Until, in desperation, I promised, 'All right! All right! I'll compromise. *Pops's* Hair Salon? Come on – if I'm going to do perms and ladies' haircuts, I can't really call it a barber's, now can I? And I have to keep a family, Pops,' I pleaded. 'I can't manage just doing men's short back and sides . . . please!' In a twinkling, everything was back in its place – shampoo bottles upright, towels neatly folded, blind pulled down and the chairs sedately in position. The flood of water didn't disappear, though. It took me ages to mop it dry enough to walk on. Maggie changed the placard to read '*Pops's* Hair Salon'. When she muttered 'I know where I'd like to shove this' I quickly propelled her out of there, in case Pops was listening.

When I told Sonya about it, saying that if it wasn't for the water everywhere I might have thought it was all a bad dream, she told me, ''Tain't no bloody dream, gal! That Pops was allus an old bugger, an' don't say I didn't warn yer! What! If the old sod were 'ere now, I'd tan 'is arse, that I would!' Then she jumped up from the seat as though taken by a fit of hiccups, rubbed her rump, and with a naughty look in her eyes told the empty air, 'Why! Yer randy ol' thing, Pops!' She spent the next half-hour looking secretly amused.

Lucky's gone missing again. ''E's like my pa-in-law,' laughed Sonya, 'lookin' fer a bit o' stray to cock 'is leg o'er!' She really is incorrigible!

Wilhelmina's in a very funny mood. She hasn't said a single word about having to go to school tomorrow, and I can't help feeling it's the lull before the storm. I don't know which way to turn with her. Tom doesn't help matters, running up and down taunting 'Willy's a fool 'cause she's going to school'. I told him I'd been making enquiries as to whether he could start after Christmas. Now they're *both* in a funny mood.

I went down to the off-licence and bought six bottles of white wine. As it's opening day for the salon tomorrow, I thought it might be nice to offer a glass to every first-day customer.

Friday, September 18th

What a day! What a glorious, wonderful, never-to-be-forgotten day! They *all* turned up! I didn't do any hair-cutting, shaves, or perms, but, oh, I did enjoy myself. I couldn't understand how word got round that I was giving away free wine, till the man from the wine shop turned up as well. 'I thought I'd come and help you celebrate the opening,' he said. There were a dozen friendly people from Casey's Court, whom I hadn't previously met, four talkative women from Rosamund Street, and all the old familiar faces. There was little Larkin, growing more excited by the minute and entertaining us with a most interesting variety of melodies; 'Likes to blow her trumpet, don't she?' remarked one of the women from Rosamund Street. Someone else said, 'Now then, Gladys! I've heard *you* rattle a few in your time!' which brought tumultuous applause from all present, though poor little Larkin went quite pink and hid herself behind Sonya. Fred and Bertha Twistle gave an interesting rendering of 'My Old Dutch' (though I do think it was rude of those two women from Rosamund Street to switch off their hearing-aids). Grandad Pitts (our Ethelbert!) and his sweetheart, Maggie, sat on the bench holding hands and gazing into each other's adoring eyes, until Mad Aggie dropped in and did a few cartwheels round the room.

'Buggered if she ain't got no bloomers on!' gasped Grandad Pitts, his attention momentarily diverted from the besotted Maggie. She shocked me to the core when, leaping to her feet, she told him, 'Ethelbert Pitts! If you'd rather feast your eyes on that crazy woman's bare arse, then feel free to do so!' With that she stormed off, with poor old Ethelbert running after her, pleading for forgiveness. I intend to take Maggie to task for using 'that word'. It has to be said that Sonya Pitts's bad influence is far-reaching. She, however, was totally oblivious of her shortcomings, bumbling about the room offering gin and Bacardi to one and all (her contribution to the wine stock, once she saw how the celebrations were going). In no time at all, there wasn't a sober expression nor straight leg in the place. A good time was had by all, and I do believe the impromptu party might have gone on for days.

However, when Smelly Kelly thrust his way into the parlour, there was blind panic. The four women from Rosamund Street thought there was a gas-leak, and, fearful that they were about to be blown to kingdom come, they made a beeline for the door. Unfortunately, with Smelly Kelly's grotesque physique still lingering in that vicinity, there was created a bottle-neck which in turn created more blind panic. 'Jesus, Mary and Joseph,' screamed another, 'I'm choking!' And suddenly everybody had slung their glasses to the floor and were fleeing in all directions. Those from Casey's Court (who recognized the source of the 'gas-leak') scrambled out of the window. Two of the Rosamund Street women managed to escape the same way, and the other two, having fainted, were carried out under the armpits of the helpful Smelly Kelly. In a matter of minutes, the place was empty – except for little Larkin, whom I found folded up in the hole beneath the barber's chair, full of Bacardi, and blissfully unaware of the storm she was blowing up which was echoing round the room

'Just look at the poor little sod,' declared Sonya, a bottle of wine in one hand and a glass of gin in the other, 'fartin' away like a good 'un!' That said, she burst into tears and began singing 'Keep the 'ome-fires burning'. She was still singing it when I struggled home with her and put her to bed.

Little Larkin put up no resistance when I pulled her out and returned her to her own parlour. 'Oh dearie me,' she kept saying, 'have I been naughty?' After I assured her that she'd been the best-behaved one there, she clapped her hands together, collapsed into her armchair, and fell straight off to sleep. I wasn't surprised to see how spick and span her home was – everything polished and in its place, and a picture of her parents taking pride of place on the mantelpiece. Sonya had already informed me that the little woman had never married, and had no living relatives. And when I looked at her, asleep in that big armchair like a tiny curled-up dormouse, I felt really sorry for her. 'You won't be lonely while I'm living next door,' I told her, covering her with a coat I found hanging on the door. Then, feeling somewhat grateful for my own brood, and vowing to be more understanding towards the children, I went back home. Lucky had returned. Tom had evidently plied both himself and the hapless dog with a concoction from every bottle, and the pair of them were contentedly snuggled up together on the scullery floor. Grandad Pitts and Maggie were in the bolt-hole, kissing and cuddling – having first removed their false teeth, which were lovingly placed one beside the other on the edge of the bunker.

I left them to it, stepped over the two drunken bodies in the scullery, made myself a welcome cuppa, and happily browsed over my appointment ledger. A full page of bookings for the next fortnight – I only hoped that they would all remember, and turn up.

Some twenty minutes later, Wilhelmina appeared, looking as if she'd gone ten rounds with Cassius Clay. 'Good Lord, Willy,' I exclaimed, 'what on earth have you been up to?' She had a technicolour eye, a split lip, and her blouse was literally in shreds. 'It's the school. It's bullies at the school, isn't it?' I demanded. 'I'll have something to say about this!' I was furious. How could Mrs Hepher let such a thing happen? Wilhelmina was obviously greatly distressed and ran upstairs sobbing.

I lost no time in getting on to the school, keeping my fingers crossed that the teaching-staff hadn't all run off the minute the bell went. Mrs Hepher was still there, and I gave her a piece of my mind.

Some five minutes later, I put the phone down, went straight upstairs, and told Wilhelmina she could go without her tea. The little brat might have explained that she received her injuries from a five-year-old child in the nursery-class. It seems Wilhelmina picked on the tiniest girl in the school – not knowing that her father is a fervent believer in children learning the art of self-defence. I feel such a fool.

Saturday, September 19th

A most satisfactory and busy day. Only one of the bookings didn't turn up. The two shampoo and sets and the gentle-wave perm arrived on time. Sonya did one of the shampoo and sets, then begged to go home. 'I'm sure I'm bloody dyin'!' she wailed, holding her head and making weird faces. She quite put the fear of God up the customers.

The woman from Rosamund Street who wanted her dark roots bleached turned up twenty minutes late. 'Me mouth feels like a cesspit!' she said, squeezing herself into the chair and moaning in agony. 'Drink an' parties don't agree with me.'

'Oh, I am sorry,' I said (I was). 'I'm very lucky, though – happy hours don't seem to have any effect on me at all.' I really believed that – until I discovered I was wearing odd shoes. And, when Mrs Farthingworth went to pay me, I was horrified to see that I must have been somewhat careless with the bleach, because she had one natural black eyebrow, and one snow-white. 'Oh, dear me, Mrs Farthingworth,' I said, wearing my best 'don't panic' smile, 'I forgot to put your free cream on.' Without further ado, I got her back in the chair and, under the pretence of dabbing her face with cream – which I blatantly claimed would shrink her wrinkles – I bleached the other eyebrow. At least she left the shop with a matching pair.

At ten thirty this evening she phoned me to make a fresh appointment. 'Do you know,' she said, sounding close to tears, 'I hadn't realized how old I was getting. Even me eyebrows is turning silver.' I'll be dying them black next week.

Wilhelmina is confined to her room. I'll swing for Tom if he doesn't stop banging on her door and yelling, 'If you cheat at snap again I'll get that baby on you!' (My nerves *are* going!)

Maggie's drifting about like a love-struck teenager. I've told her, though, that if she will insist on wearing those bright blue and red striped knickers she bought at the market, she's asking for trouble.

Sunday, September 20th

I've made arrangements with Maggie to pay her twenty pounds a week off the money I owe her (which we both calculate to be six hundred pounds). It's lovely being independent at long last, and seeing my list of customers grow by the day. I'm getting much better and more confident – even Sonya says so.

That wretched Wilhelmina! I let her come down to go to the outside lavvy, and she scarpered. We searched high and low for hours, and couldn't find head nor tail of her. At five o'clock a police-officer brought her home (it was the very same one who'd come out when the green-eyed monster tried to get into the house). 'I think you should take a good look at yourself, Mrs Jolly,' he said, having apparently heard about the party we had here the other day. 'You're not setting a very good example to these children of yours, are you? I understand this poor girl's been locked in her bedroom for days. I'll say no more at this point, other than to remind you of the laws in this country regarding cruelty to children. Oh, I know they can drive you to distraction at times, Mrs Jolly, but it's only boredom that causes it, you know. The thing to do is get them interested in something or another. Now, take me and my five-year-old daughter. The other day she was set upon at school by a bully three times her size. It was only her keen interest in self-defence that saved her from a leathering.' He was amazed when Wilhelmina disappeared upstairs like greased lightning. 'My word!' he exclaimed. 'And she told me you nearly broke both her legs!' He gave me another warning – if somewhat half-hearted now – and off he went.

Monday, September 21st

An ambulance dashed into Casey's Court today and drew up right next door. In a matter of minutes the whole street was out, to see two figures muffled up in blankets being rushed into the back of the ambulance. 'It's all that bonking!' declared Granny Grabber, clutching a fistful of Mad Aggie's rear end. (Folks took little notice of Aggie jumping up and down, shouting, 'Ooha! Wahey!' They're used to it).

Little Larkin kept saying, 'Poor things – oh, dearie me!' Maggie and Ethelbert held hands and gazed into each other's eyes. And Sonya gave them both a shrivelling look.

'Look at them silly buggers! Don't they know *their* bonking days are over?' I told her not to be so cruel. (I feel exactly the same about *my* 'bonking days'.)

Talking of which, I had a bunch of flowers delivered to the door today. There was a card from Barny Singleton, saying he wasn't putting up the white flag, because he wasn't too pleased about having lost the husbands of four Rosamund Street women to me, so if I didn't let him take me out to dinner on Saturday evening he'd cut his charges to the bone and engage me in price-warfare. Could I afford that? As I could not, I sent a note over with Tom saying that, in the circumstances, I had better accept his invitation. Back came the arrangement that he would pick me up at eight thirty on the evening in question. 'Has he got a thingie as well?' Tom asked. I gave him a ticking off, whereupon he went off into the back yard, sulking. 'I expect it's bigger than mine,' he shouted, ''cause he's got taller legs.' I'm still trying to figure that one out.

I must put Saturday evening and Barny Singleton right out of my mind, or I'll never get through the week.

The phone rang at half past five this morning. Maggie came falling down the stairs in her new heart-bedecked nightie, eyes closed and still asleep. 'Who is it? Who was it, Jessy?' She seemed almost frantic.

'It was only a wrong number,' I assured her.

'Thank goodness!' she gasped. 'I thought they'd found me!'

It was two hours later, when we'd risen again, fully awake and fit to do battle with the flying toast, that it suddenly dawned on me what Maggie had said. So, when we'd managed to pin two slices of toast to our plates, I asked her, 'Maggie . . . what did you mean this morning, when you said you thought they'd found you?'

'Did I say that?'

'You most certainly did.'

'How silly. I've no idea why. I must have been talking in my sleep.' I'm not surprised she didn't know what she was talking about at that God-forsaken hour. That caller has a lot to answer for, I thought, looking in the mirror at the two kangaroo-pouches beneath my eyes.

I thought I'd have a quick look through the paper before Sonya arrived to commandeer it. And there was that Currie woman again. 'We must all eat less fat!' she pronounced, her photograph grinning up at me. It gave me a little squirm of pleasure to prop up her face next to the milk bottle, where she could see me shamelessly layering half a pound of butter over my toast.

Wednesday, September 23rd

There was a long heart-breaking letter from Tiffany in the post this morning. It was bordering on suicidal, so I decided to have a stern heart-to-heart with her. When I got through it was himself who answered. 'I'm glad it's you!' I said. 'I'll come straight to the point! You're carrying on with that harlot next door, and breaking your wife's heart. You swine! You ought to be locked up, the pair of you!'

I was delighted when he was somewhat taken aback. Then horrified when I heard the quiet remark, 'This is the plumber, come to fix a leak. I'm sorry, but there's nobody else in.' I dropped that phone as if it was white-hot. I never have liked telephones. They get you into all manner of trouble.

I don't like the way Wilhelmina's behaving. She's too polite – it's very worrying! Also, Tom's taken to locking himself in the loo for ages at a time. (I'm not cut out to understand children. They frighten me. Whenever my back's turned, I have this terrible feeling they're just waiting to pounce.)

Maggie asked me to perm her hair. I told her that she already had naturally pretty waves. And I warned her several times that a perm would not make her more attractive to Ethelbert. Hadn't he fallen in love with her the way she was? 'I want to turn him on!' she insisted, so I permed her hair. Later she cried like a baby, when Ethelbert said he'd seen better drain-cleaners. They had their first quarrel. And boy, was it a humdinger! I'm writing this in bed. It's midnight, and Maggie stubbornly refuses to come out of her bunker. I can hear her now – throwing things at the marauding tomcats.

It's not easy being an employer. Sonya and I had our first disagreement this morning. First of all, she turned up ten minutes late. ''Tain't my fault!' she argued. 'Grandad Pitts 'as tekken to doing exercises to improve his physique, or so he says! That's all very well . . . but 'e were at the bugger all night! I'm tellin' yer, Jessy, I never got a wink o' sleep.'

Later, I heard a different tale from Maggie. According to what Ethelbert told her, it was *he* who hadn't had a wink of sleep, on account of 'some bloody peculiar noises comin' fro' Sonya's room, well into the early hours'. He described the noises as being 'some'at akin to them squeals an' eerie sounds that cats mek when they're matin''. Three times he knocked on Sonya's door, to ask if she was all right: 'I were convinced the poor lass were deep in a nightmare!' I can imagine how hurt he was when she shouted out 'Piss orf!'

'Y'know,' he told Maggie, with some paternal concern, 'since our lad ran off an' left her an' she moved in wi' me, that poor Sonya's been prone to tirrible bad dreams. Oh, aye! Some nights she moans an' groans just as if she were 'avin' a tussle wi' somebody . . . it's right unnervin', so it is.'

'Look here, Sonya,' I told her, in a slack period, 'if I'm going to pay you like a proper assistant, you must behave in a professional manner. Arrive on time, and wear that white overall I gave you. *I* have to.'

'Stuff yer bloody overall! I ain't workin' fer no dentist!' In a huff, she threw down her tools and marched off. I wouldn't have minded, but she was half way through Mrs Bullock's blue rinse at the time.

'You come right back here,' I shouted, leaving Maggie and Tom in charge as I dashed up the street after her.

When I rushed into her parlour, she was bent double in the chair, head in hands and sobbing her heart out. 'Aw, Sonya, I'm sorry,' I said, putting my arm round her shoulder. 'I should have realized there was something wrong. What is it, eh? You can tell me.' I hated to see her so upset. Sonya had become like a sister to me, and, whatever her failings, I loved her.

'Me whole life's buggered up,' she sobbed, 'an' I don't know what to do next.'

'How can your whole life be "buggered up"? Don't be silly, Sonya. What is it? Are you ill? Have you seen the doctor? Have you lost one of your favourite clients? If that's the case, it'll be for the better. Just look at that Doreen Desiree, who stormed out of the salon when her curly perm wouldn't take. We lost *her*, didn't we? Then, two days later, she was back – bald as a mole and threatening to sue me. Look at her now! Chuffed to bits with that curly wig I sold her.'

'Naw. It ain't nowt to do wi' any o' me clients. I'm fittin' them in well, next to the hours I work fer you. It's just that . . . well, I'm afeared I *will* lose 'em, now.'

'Why should you?' I remembered what Maggie had told me about the way Grandad Pitts had been kept awake, and how he'd banged on Sonya's door, thinking she was having a nightmare. 'Are you afraid your father-in-law might find out what's going on?'

'Naw! Naw, Jessy . . .'tain't that.' She straightened up and looked at me with big sore red eyes. 'I reckon I'm in the puddin' club!' she said, and launched off into a fresh spate of bawling.

'Good God, Sonya,' I gasped, the two monsters in mind, 'that's terrible!'

'I've done the lot, Jessy,' she said. 'I've got mesel' one o' them exercise bikes, an' I've spent hours on it, till me

111

back aches an' me legs feel like jelly, floggin' mesel' 'alf to death till all hours o' the night!' So that was what Grandad Pitts had heard. 'I've sat in a bath o' water so bloody 'ot that me toes 'ave curled, an' I've polished off four bottles o' gin. None of it works. I'm still up the bloody spout.'

'How can you be sure? Have you seen a doctor?' I asked, clutching at straws.

'I don't need no bloody doctor to tell me that. I'm in the puddin' club . . . I just know it.' Poor Sonya. I had no idea what to say to pacify her. I just listened while she got it all off her chest – how she didn't even know who the father was (it could have been any one of at least sixteen) and what Grandad Pitts would say to having a bawling pink lump about the place. And how many of her men-friends would come round when she was big as a barge and waddling round like a duck.

I left her with a fresh brew of tea, and told her I'd be back later. 'I don't know what I'd do wi'out you,' she said, giving me a bear-hug. 'Yer a bloody good pal, Jessica Jolly!'

When I got back to the salon, Tom had squirted shaving-cream up the walls, and Maggie was chasing him all over the place. Mrs Bullock's blue rinse had dripped everywhere. She looked like a stick of Blackpool rock. 'Get me out of here!' she shouted. 'It's like a madhouse. I'm never coming back.' She changed her mind, once I'd cleaned her up and booked four free appointments. 'We all have our off-days,' she smiled, going out of the door in a brilliant blue haze. What a day!

There was a team of Council officials trampling up and down Casey's Court today. They all had little clip-boards and were busily scribbling things down on them. One of the officials was foolish enough to knock on Grandad Pitts's door to ask a few questions. The answers could be heard from one end of Casey's Court to the other. 'Yer can stuff that bloody board up yer arse, my man! An' if yer don't get the hell outta Casey's Court this soddin' minute I'll do it for yer!' He pointed his air-rifle at the fellow's tender parts. 'Go on! Piss orf, I tell yer! Else ye'll not *'ave* an arse ter call yer bloody own!'

'Really, Mr Pitts!' The man looked up and down the street, his face unnaturally pink. 'Must you be so loud and abusive? Where's your pride, man?' When he won no favourable response, the poor fellow retreated with a semblance of dignity until Grandad Pitts came out on to the flagstones, when his courage deserted him and he took to his heels and disappeared away round the corner as if the devil was after him.

'An' don't come back!' Grandad Pitts yelled after him. 'Else yer wife'll be wantin' ter know where *your* bloody "pride" has gone!'

I had the carpenter in today to fit a bench along one wall where customers could wait in comfort. The trouble was, he had a wonky eye. I didn't notice until after he'd gone that the bench legs were shorter at one end than at the other. It looked more like a slide than a bench. Tom thought it was great. He spent the best part of the afternoon piling Lucky on to one end, then, after giving the terrified animal a mighty push, he'd rush to the other end and catch him. 'I'll come and see to it, when I've time,' promised the carpenter. (It was a pity I'd paid him in cash.) I would have wedged the low end up, but the legs were bolted to the floor.

Sonya didn't come to work today. I was kept really busy, so I sent Maggie out to see if she was all right. Apparently, she'd gone out. 'What took you three hours before you came back to tell me that?' I asked Maggie. I wasn't unduly surprised when she explained how Ethelbert had shown her his artefact collection, and she, being keen to appear interested, had taken a long time examining them.

'They're not much use, but they're really quite pretty,' she said. Well I never!

Saturday, September 26th

I didn't sleep a wink all night what with one thing and another. Worry about Sonya, and excitement about going out with Barny tonight. And when I reckoned up the week's takings, minus Maggie's twenty pounds and thirty pounds to Sonya, I was left with sixty-four pounds. Marvellous! I made an appointment with the rep to deliver another small consignment on Tuesday, so the cost of that – together with the fifteen pounds I spent on a dress for tonight – will eat half of my profit away. But, slowly and surely, I'm getting there – that's all that matters.

At two o'clock Sonya came to see me. 'Come on, gal,' she said, making an effort to put the semblance of a smile on her face. 'Just 'cause I'm down in the dumps don't mean ter say I can't wash 'n' set me best mate's 'air when she's goin' on a date! Get thisel' in that parlour! I'll 'ave yer lookin' like Princess Diana in no time!' I was so pleased to have her bossing me about again that I laughed out loud and gave her a peck on the cheek. 'Gerroff!' she shouted, marching ahead of me into the parlour. 'Anybody'd think yer ain't seen me fer a year or two!' It was good to have her back.

While she set about transforming me into a beauty queen, I brought up the subject of her 'little problem'. 'Hmh! 'Tain't no *little* problem, Jessica,' she said, the frown returning to her homely face, 'it's a bloody *big* one . . . an' short o' jumpin' off Tinkers Bridge, I dunno what to do.' After a deal of persuasion, she agreed to go and see the doctor, mainly because 'I've tried one o' them self-pregnancy tests, an' there's bugger all 'appens! It don't show I am, an' it don't show I ain't!'

'What does it do, then?' I asked her.

'It bloody *melts*,' she said, 'an' it don't say nowt about that in the instructions.' It was agreed that she would go to the doctor's first thing on Monday morning. 'But I'm tellin' yer, Jessica, I've seen nowt fer two months, an' ooh, I feel that sick of a mornin'. What else can it be, eh? You tell me that!'

I had to admit, it did sound ominous. I would have spent a while trying to cheer her by outlining the merits and wonder of having a young person to look up to you for everything. But in all truth, I couldn't bring myself to lie. 'Just think, Sonya,' I said instead, trying to cheer her up another way, 'if it's a little girl she'll probably look just like you.'

'Oh, aye!' came the retort. 'An' she might be a bloody Chinaman as well . . . or a Paddy! Or she might be a shade dark, I shouldn't wonder!' She was not cheered by my helpful remarks. 'Aw, look 'ere, Jessica. I'm thirty-nine year old . . . forty in a few weeks. For Gawd's sake, let's look at it in the light o' day. What would I do wi' a bundle o' pink flesh 'n' blood? It don't matter whether the poor little bugger looks like me or the Queen o'

115

soddin' Sheba, 'cause the plain truth o' the matter is I ain't fit ter be no mother, an' you know it as well as I do. I'm a slag . . . a tart, a prostitute, if yer wants ter put it truthfully. An' folks like me 'ave no bloody right fotchin' babies into the world. On top o' which, I wouldn't 'ave the slightest idea what the 'ell ter do wi' it!' Coming from Sonya, that was quite a speech, and when I pointed out that there was no need to put herself down like that she threw a big friendly arm round my shoulder and, in that endearing way she has of displaying affection, shook me till my teeth rattled. 'Bless yer ol' 'eart, Jessica gal!' she said with a suspicious tremble in her voice. 'Yer a real mate . . . but yer can only see the best side o' me. I were a real 'ell-raiser when I were a snotty-nosed kid in raggy pants . . . an' I've growed up a bad 'un. There's nowt yer can say ter alter that. Nowt at all!' In spite of Sonya's self-confessed failings, she was not 'a bad 'un', and I had to say so. With a shrug of her shoulders and a great mountainous sigh, she replied, 'Aye, well. That's right grand o' yer ter say so, lass. But I'm not one ter fool mesel'. There's quality, an' there's cheap rubbish, an' I know which I am.' Having secured the last word on the subject, she spent a full two hours titivating my hair, until, at half past four, she held the mirror up in front of me. 'What d'yer think?' she asked, looking decidedly pleased with herself.

When I saw the reflection in that mirror, I was astonished. A ravishing redhead looked back at me with wide hazel eyes. I had no idea my hair had such a deep fiery glow – and how on earth had she coaxed it into those extravagantly feminine curls, caught up in a gentle bunch at the top of my head with teased-out wisps cascading down around my neck and face? I looked so pretty. I *felt* beautiful. 'Oh, Sonya, you really do have an artistic streak in you, do you know that?' I gasped. 'And how clever you are with your fingers.'

The spell was somehow broken when she retorted with a loud guffaw, 'Aye . . . that's why all the fellas keep comin' back! I'm off 'ome now, but I'll be back ter mek yer face up an' get yer ready at eight o'clock,' she said in spite of my assurance that I really could manage to dress and make myself up. Somehow, the thought of having three inches of creme-puff and colour-stick plastered on my face did nothing to boost my confidence.

Maggie and I got the tea, and ensured that the children were washed and in their pyjamas, ready for an early night. There were cries of protest, and assurances from Wilhelmina that 'if you let me play out longer, I promise I won't run away'.

Maggie put her foot down. 'You will,' she accused, 'and I have no intention of chasing all over the place after you, my girl!' Sentiments I fully endorsed.

'You can watch the television until Maggie says it's bedtime,' I told her, 'or play a game of snap with Tom.'

She wasn't at all keen on that idea because, as she so quaintly put it, 'He's no fun any more. All he wants to do is measure his thingie.' I considered it my bounden duty to explain to Tom that if he didn't stop indulging in such ridiculous pastimes, he'd wake up one morning to find his 'thingie' had dropped off.

'Don't be silly,' he replied, with a patronizing shake of his dark curly head, 'it can't drop off. I know, because Bobby Brewster told me it goes right through your body, and comes out on your face where your nose is! I bet you didn't know that, did you?' No, I didn't.

'When you're old enough,' I said, avoiding the issue, 'I'll explain all about the bits that you're built with.'

He explained with extreme patience that I needn't

bother, because Bobby Brewster had already told him. 'And he knows *everything*,' Tom said proudly, '*and* he knows how to spell bum!'

I was getting out of my depth. 'Maggie,' I said, 'if he says another word about this know-all Bobby Brewster, he's to be put straight to bed!' He suddenly found an interest in cutting out the pictures in his comic.

At eight o'clock, when there was a knock on the door, I thought it might be Sonya, come to make me up. How could I explain, without hurting her feelings, that her idea of looking glamorous was really not mine? I could never see myself opening the door to Barny Singleton looking like a colourful totem-pole. And how could I give him the come-on look from two eyes that resembled a surprised panda's?

It was not Sonya at the door, but Grandad Pitts, come calling on Maggie. 'I'll baby-sit with her,' he said, thrusting past me into the waiting arms of his doting lover. 'Hello, sweetheart.'

'Hello, my angel,' she cooed. Then they smacked their lips together. It was like two shunters colliding in the goods yard.

'Where's Sonya?' I asked, when his mouth was free.

'Oh, she ain't comin' down. She says as yer ter 'ave a good time an' yer can tell 'er all about it tomorrer!' He went on to explain that she was having an early night with an aspirin. (I hated myself for wondering whether it might be an *Irish* aspirin.)

At twenty minutes past eight, I took a last look at myself in the long Victorian mirror that old Pops had left behind. I was quite pleased with the end result. 'You'll pass, Jessica Jolly,' I told myself, eyeing my reflection up and down. It did present a pretty picture, even if I did say so myself. The new dress I'd treated myself to was worth

118

every penny of the fifteen pounds I'd paid for it. It was a lovely shade of cornflower blue, with scalloped neckline, nipped-in waist and full swirling skirt which fell to calf-length. The cream high-heeled shoes looked just right with it, and the slim blue clutch-bag completed the ensemble beautifully. I had been sparing with the make-up, using only a little dusting of powder and the merest suggestion of russet eye-shadow, with one generous layer of black mascara. The lipstick was deep pink, and the ear-rings just small circles of blue.

'Oh, I say!' Maggie exclaimed when I entered the room, feeling like a teenager on my first date, and hating myself for the butterflies fluttering my insides. 'You do look lovely. Doesn't she look lovely?' she asked Grandad Pitts, who lifted his head from her neck, cast a weary eye over me and declared, 'Aye, she does . . . but I 'ave ter say that I only 'ave eyes fer you, my sweet.' Whereupon he made a grab for her and helped himself to another gobstopper.

'Ethelbert! Not in front of the children!' Maggie cautioned him, and was put down quite nicely by Wilhelmina, who piped in, 'It's all right. You can kiss and cuddle if you like', Tom adding, ''Course you can! Bobby Brewster says his mam and dad do it all the time . . . only *he*'s allowed to watch!'

At that point there came a knock on the door. Before I could get there, Wilhelmina shot through my legs and yanked the door open, to tell Barny Singleton with wide eyes, 'She's been upstairs for *hours* getting herself all pretty for you. Maggie told Grandad Pitts that she wouldn't be surprised if my mother was looking for another husband, because she's besotted with you. But me and Tom don't want you for our daddy. Tom says

119

you've got a bigger thingie than him, and you want to throw us out on the street!'

I do not regret the crafty kick on the shins I gave her. And she can sulk all she likes.

The evening started out well. Barny was so handsome in black trousers and grey-speckled jacket, with an open-necked white shirt beneath and a clutch of long dark hairs peeping out at the throat. When he gazed down at me with those eyes – so darkly beautiful they should never belong to any man – I felt myself turn to jelly. Then, when he murmured with that gorgeous crooked smile, 'How lovely you look,' and took me by the arm to lovingly place me in his car, I positively melted.

When we entered the restaurant and were shown to a candle-lit dinner table, I could feel people's eyes on us, and I felt proud to be escorted by such a virile and handsome fellow. I know from the looks on their faces that there were plenty of women present who'd change places in a flash.

Once we were seated, Barny's dark smouldering eyes never left mine. Placing his long lean fingers over my trembling hand, he whispered, 'Did you see the look on those men's faces? I bet they'd give their right arms to be in my shoes tonight.' Then, leaning over the table, he lifted my hand and, placing it to his mouth, he touched his warm soft lips to the palm. I could hardly breathe. 'You really are a beautiful woman, Jessica,' he said, 'but I'm sure you've been told that before.' I hadn't. 'Later,' he murmured, 'we could drive up to the top of the moors . . . it's a lovely view from there. Then perhaps we might go for a stroll in the moonlight?' I was so excited I couldn't keep a limb still.

He ordered a bottle of best rosé and began explaining how silly we'd been to start off at loggerheads – that I was right, of course, there was room enough for the two of us to make a decent living without fighting for customers – there were enough to go round. In fact, I found myself feeling a bit of a rotter for having come into his home territory and, quite without conscience, having taken his valuable customers (fifteen to date). I began thinking how badly I'd judged Barny Singleton – he was not the ogre I'd painted him. He was not ruthless. Nor would he employ devious tricks to get me to pack up my business. In fact, I began wondering how I would feel if some perfect stranger had muscled in and set herself up against me. I'd be more than justified in being furious, if she was drawing customers away from me left right and centre. I began to see myself as he must see me – and I did not like the pushy, grasping image that presented itself. In fact, the more wine I drank, and the more he made love to me with his voice, with the lingering suggestive touch of his hand, the more I could see what a blatantly ruthless person I'd become. And the more I despised myself.

The waiter knew Barny quite well. 'Hello, Mr Singleton,' he said, flashing a broad white smile at my escort and handing him the menu. 'So nice to see you enjoying yourself – and in the company of such a beautiful lady.' I took to him right away. 'It's the best thing, you know,' he went on seriously, 'to leave the working week and its troubles behind, and enjoy yourself.' He turned to me. 'Poor Mr Singleton,' he said. 'I suppose you know all about his troubles?'

At this point, Barny made an effort to stop him. 'No, no,' he protested, 'the lady doesn't want to hear about my troubles, John!' But I did, if only because I was hopelessly head over heels in love with the man – and might later get the chance to console him in a more intimate fashion.

'No, you go on, John,' I encouraged, bestowing upon Barny my most enigmatic smile, and lovingly caressing his fingers. 'Mr Singleton's troubles are my troubles also.' My heartfelt words so moved my handsome Barny that he dropped his head into his hands and groaned.

John was a wonderful friend to Barny – and a wonderful talker. Out spilled the whole deluge regarding 'poor Mr Singleton's dreadful trouble' and the cause of it: 'some awful woman who's moved here from the south, and is trying to bankrupt him'. I was subjected to John's revelations of how poor Mr Singleton had almost been driven to drink by this 'po-faced and unfeminine tyrant'. 'If you ask me,' John confided, 'I think the repugnant creature and her ill-assorted family should be run out of town, and never be allowed to come back.' But our Mr Singleton had it all in hand now. John explained how she was about to get her come-uppance. 'She won't get the better of Mr Singleton!' he declared with a smug grimace. 'Our Mr Singleton has a way with the ladies, being so handsome and charming. He's going to engage his every wile in bringing this vile and vindictive woman to heel.' His methods included such interesting tactics as informing the Council on her every move, getting certain reps to boycott her place of business, and if all else failed employing his charm and looks to woo her over to his way of thinking. 'He's going to flatter her – wine and dine her, and walk her . . . in . . . the . . . moonlight!' enthused John the mouth. And only at that late point, when out had tumbled the words 'wine and dine', did the penny begin to drop. The part about walking in the moonlight stuttered painfully out while he swivelled his bright little eyes towards the haggard face of 'Mr Singleton' – who merely groaned again, and slowly nodded his head as the light dawned on John's horrified features.

In the same instant, my melon arrived. I never did have a very good aim. So, when smarmy Barny ducked, it went sailing past him to catch a poor unsuspecting waiter full in the tail-end as he bent to serve his customers. 'Oh my!' he said, straightening up and looking about with starry eyes. 'Come out, come out, whoever you are!'

Clapping his hand to his mouth, John cried, 'Oh, you shouldn't have done that. He'll be completely useless for the rest of the week.'

As I ran for the exit, I could hear Barny calling out, 'Come back, Jessica!' But I was away in a taxi before he came rushing out, and though my eyes were blurred by tears and running mascara I saw him standing in the middle of the road looking totally dejected. 'Good!' I murmured. 'You're a swine, Barny Singleton!' And all swines deserve to end up wallowing in their own mud.

I guessed that was him knocking at the door at ten o'clock. I let him knock and went straight to bed. I hate him!

Maggie made no comment when she saw me, other than to remark on her own good fortune in having found 'my darling Ethelbert. He's a gentleman and knows how to treat a lady.' I shall tell her tomorrow – in the kindest possible way – that a woman of her age should not be seen to display a necklace of love-bites. Or – if, as I strongly suspect, Grandad Pitts took his teeth out – love-*sucks*.

It was two A.M. when I was awakened by frantic banging on the front door. 'The cheek of the fellow!' I told Maggie. 'Devious, two-faced Don Juan!'

The nearest thing to hand was Maggie's Jeremiah under the bed. 'Give it here!' she said, and, against my protests, she opened the window and emptied the pot over him just as he stepped back to look up. 'Clear off, you conceited

123

Casanova!' she yelled, and then shrank in horror when she saw that it was Grandad Pitts.

'Ooh, yer little tiger!' he cooed, licking his lips and winking at her.

'Oh, Maggie!' I said, disgusted.

'What d'you mean,' she glared, 'looking at me like that and saying "Oh, Maggie!" in that tone of voice. '*I'm* the one who should be mortified! I've spent a whole week fermenting that concoction in my Jeremiah.'

'Concoction?' I was lost. But oh, how relieved when she explained that she and Ethelbert had been following an old recipe for punch!

'It was going to be a surprise for our engagement party. Now I'll have to start all over again.'

The alley-cats liked it anyway, because when I leaned out of the window to ask what he wanted at this time of morning there were dozens of little pink tongues lapping at the pavement. Little Larkin was at the door in her mob-cap and nightie. 'Oh dearie me!' she was crying nervously. 'Whatever is it?' The night was rent by such impressive cymbal-clapping that the lights went on up and down Casey's Court. I expect they thought the circus was in town.

Grandad Pitts was not easily deterred. He stood his ground. 'It's Sonya!' he called up. 'They've rushed 'er orf ter the infirmary!' (They do say it never rains but it pours.)

Sunday, September 27th

I was up bright and early this morning (well, perhaps not so bright). Maggie had kept me awake half the night, screaming and shouting in her sleep that 'I'll kill myself before I'll let you shut me away'. When I went to gently

124

wake her up, she grabbed my arm and began sobbing, 'Oh, Ethelbert, I do love you so. Don't let them get me . . . let's elope to Gretna Green and never come back!' Then, before I could stop her (she's as strong as a lion – I expect it's all that digging that's developed her muscles), she yanked me on top of her and slapped her mouth all over my face. It was awful – like being beaten to death with a wet flannel.

I couldn't wake her up. But Wilhelmina did the trick by jumping on top of her and shouting, 'Rally the troops! Rally the troops!' She was out of that bed in two seconds flat. In another two, she was crouched outside in the bunker with her tin hat on, having steamrollered every obstacle in her path, including me and Wilhelmina. By this time, Tom was awake and, in the best tradition of all obnoxious little creatures, had messed his pants and hidden himself under the bed.

'Come out, you silly little fool!' I said, holding my nose.

'No! I won't!' came the reply, his two saucer eyes staring at me from the murky depths. 'There's monsters.' It didn't pacify him when I promised that the only monster – besides himself and his sister – was bent double in the bunker.

Two hours later, at six A.M., order was restored. As there seemed little point in going back to bed, we engaged in battle with the toaster, made a pot of tea and, afterwards, all fell asleep downstairs. Lucky woke us up by scrabbling at the back door.

I asked Maggie whether there was anything she'd like to confide in me, since she seemed so troubled in her sleep. She denied that there was anything wrong and moved on to other things. 'I'll watch the children,' she said, bustling about in the kitchen. 'You go off and see Sonya. I'm sure Ethelbert will be along to keep me company.'

As usual, Sonya was a real tonic. 'Am I glad to see you!' she declared, propped up at a most uncomfortable-looking angle.

'What are you lying all twisted like that for?' I asked.

I felt a fool when she shouted for everyone to hear, ''Cause the buggers 'ave sat me on this bloody bed-pan, an' it ain't natural!' I was curious to know what was unnatural about a bed-pan. ''Cause the place is short of equipment an' they've only got *fellers'* bed-pans. It's got this great hollow lump on the end . . . fer their spout, d'yer see? Only I reckon that student nurse sat me on it back ter front, 'cause it's stickin' up me arse!' She really did look pained. 'It's all that Maggie Thatcher's fault! I bet she don't 'ave none o' this trouble when *she's* in soddin' 'orspital!' When I pointed out that she mustn't shout and swear like that, disturbing the other patients, she nearly exploded. 'Bugger *them*!' she yelled, waving a fist about. 'What about *me*, eh? Be a good 'un,' she pleaded, 'fotch somebody ter get me orf this contraption.'

I went in all haste in search of help. Sonya was right. The nurse had put her on the bed-pan back to front. 'I'm sorry,' she said, 'but we're so short-staffed, we're having to do twice the work.'

Sonya took some pacifying, feeling 'cut in bloody 'alf' as she did. 'Me 'eart bleeds fer yer,' she told the nurse, 'an' I know it's not your fault . . . but I 'ope yer more careful wi' them old bed-ridden folks. Poor buggers! I'm glad I'm not one, else I'd be 'avin' nightmares about which end ye'd be forcin' me porridge in!'

After the little nurse had scuttled away, Sonya related the events leading up to her dash to the infirmary. It seemed she'd felt really bad all day, with pains in her stomach, not able to keep anything down, and 'me insides feelin' like a ship on the ocean . . . up an' down . . . up an' down . . . dippin' an' risin' . . . dippin' an' risin''. (I didn't feel too well myself.) 'In the end, I 'ad such grippin' pains that I sent the ol' feller ter the tripe shop ter phone the ambulance. 'E were after fotchin' you, but I telled 'im I didn't want yer worried, like.' A broad smile spread across her face. 'Guess what?' she asked, looking very pleased with herself. When I refrained from the guessing game, she threw her arms up in the air and shouted, 'I ain't up the bloody spout!' I was as pleased as she was. 'Yer see, they think I've got this blocked viaduct – it's that that's been givin' me trouble.'

I had visions of a great bridge, all clogged up like a dam. 'Sonya,' I said quietly, 'I've never heard of a "blocked viaduct" . . . are you sure that's what they told you?'

She was adamant. 'I ain't bloody deaf. That's what they telled me right enough. Oh, except ter say they weren't sure, like . . . an' they 'ad ter do more tests. Any road, them pills they gave me took the pain away. So they must know what they're on about, eh?'

She was beginning to get worried, I could see. I didn't want to be responsible for her discharging herself – I knew she would, if the mood took her – so I assured her at once, 'Of course they know what they're on about. They found out you weren't pregnant, didn't they? And now they've to find out why you've been in such discomfort.'

She readily agreed, and a look of relief swept over her face as she laughed, 'Aye! Yer right, gal! That young doctor as come round ter me last night . . .'e were a bit of all right. I'll enjoy bein' given the once-over by that feller!'

Inevitably, we got on to the subject of Barny Singleton. 'Did yer 'ave a lovely time, gal?' she asked with wide eager eyes. ''E's that 'andsome! Did 'e mek love ter yer afterwards? Did 'e, eh?' When I told her what really happened, the bed trembled. 'The bugger!' she shouted, sitting bolt upright. 'The two-faced devious sod!' I couldn't agree more. To calm her down, I changed the subject to Maggie's nightmare. Sonya had a suitable answer to all of Maggie's problems. 'It's that bloody ol' feller o' mine! Thinks 'e's Clark Gable, 'e does.'

I wasn't altogether convinced that Grandad Pitts was the root of Maggie's problems – there really was something deeper troubling her, I knew. 'You could be right,' I told Sonya nevertheless, thinking it less bother to go along with her.

''Course I'm right, gal! Well! I mean, just look at the pair on 'em! There's 'im, tryin' ter clean a chimney wi' a worn-out flue-brush, an' there's poor Maggie, who must be that frustrated.' I wasn't keen to continue that line of conversation either.

At that point, the sister came along and asked whether I'd mind leaving. 'She is still under observation, you see.' We cleared up the matter of Sonya's 'blocked viaduct' as well. It was a blocked bile duct. 'But that's only a possibility,' explained the sister. 'We won't really know until further examinations have been made.'

As I left, Sonya's familiar voice boomed out behind me, 'I'm stayin' awake when yer do these 'ere examinations. I've 'eard what goes on once yer knock a patient out cold. Well, yer ain't 'avin' no 'undreds o' students gawpin' up *my* arse, I can tell yer!' That's our Sonya.

When I got home, Tom was in a terrible state. 'He's broken his lego set,' explained Maggie.

'Yes, and it's all your fault!' he told me. It had become his favourite pastime to blame me for every misfortune that befell him.

'Oh, now,' I said, 'you can't blame me, not this time. I wasn't here.'

'No, but I was thinking about you when it happened!' he bawled. I give up.

Three times Barny Singleton rang. 'Keep off this line!' I told him. 'We have nothing to say to each other!' I don't think I'll ever forgive him.

'What are you going to do about him?' Maggie wanted to know.

'I'm going to steal every last one of his customers.' That was my intention. And I didn't care if he went broke.

'That's being ruthless!' Maggie was horrified, until I told her how we'd all been described by him as an 'ill-assorted' family. 'He deserves everything he gets!' she said. That's exactly how I feel.

Monday, September 28th

It's been a fairly quiet day, thank goodness!

When I was washing down the salon window early this morning, Barny Singleton emerged from the house with the gorgeous brunette on his arm. When he saw me looking, he blew a kiss in my direction before roaring away up the street with her perched beside him, looking like a film-star. As if I care!

Tiffany's husband rang. Did I know that Tiffany had a lover? No, I did not. 'Well, she has,' he moaned, 'and I'm at my wits' end.' I feel like Marje Proops.

Wilhelmina seems to be settling in at school (fingers crossed). And Tom was good as gold all day. I gave him the job of sweeping up the hair-cuttings. He made a lovely wig for Lucky.

Maggie helped me by doing the shampooing, and we were all so busy that the day just fled by.

This evening, I went with Grandad Pitts to see Sonya.

'Me insides feel like a skating-rink,' she moaned, bursting into tears when she revealed that she might have to have a hysterectomy. 'They tek all yer female bits out,' she said, dabbing at her eyes with the corner of the sheet. 'I'll never feel like a woman again.'

Both Grandad Pitts and I made every attempt to pacify her. 'Don't be so bloody daft, lass!' he told her, scorning her fears that she'd 'never feel like a woman again'. 'Time ter start worryin' is when yer gets 'air on yer chest.' I don't think that helped much.

Tuesday, September 29th

At five P.M. the carpenter still hadn't been to make the bench level. 'Let me 'ave a go at it,' Grandad Pitts suggested, rolling up his shirt-sleeves. While I was frantically searching for a kindly way to discourage him, Maggie came to the rescue.

'No, tiddly-winks,' she said, wrapping her arms about him and swallowing his ear, 'you save your strength till later.' The look she gave him was quite devastating. At any rate, it had a peculiar effect on our Ethelbert, because he made this odd choking noise and collapsed into the chair. It was only after he turned a ghastly shade of maroon that we realized he'd swallowed his teeth.

Tom and Wilhelmina looked on quite mesmerized while Maggie held Ethelbert upside down by the ankles, thumping her fist on his back while he coughed and spluttered. 'What are they doing?' Tom asked Wilhelmina.

'I expect they're bonking,' she replied (little Miss Know-all). Talking of which, there are rumours abroad that the pair from next door have been sent to a rest-home.

Sonya isn't allowed any visitors until tomorrow. She's had her exploratory operation, and is 'as comfortable as can be expected,' they said.

Wednesday, September 30th

A gypsy came to the door this morning. Old and wrinkled she was, with big black eyes and one of those faces that make you feel sad. 'Can I tell your fortune, dearie?' she asked. I gave her two pound coins, but she insisted on having her palm crossed with silver, so I put 50p into it. She didn't give me the two pound coins back, though.

'I see a tall, incredibly handsome dark stranger,' she said. I knew straight away she meant Barny Singleton. 'Watch him! He's a divill!' There . . . I knew it! She also told me that I'd had a recent bereavement. How clever of her! She means Vernon Jolly, of course, I thought. 'It was a sad business,' she went on, 'but he who has gone before left you with hope for the future.' (Oh . . . she meant old Pops.) Then she went on to tell me that she could see the wind of change blowing my way (that must be Larkin hanging out her washing), and that some time during the next few weeks there would be revealed to me news of a shocking nature. 'It will involve someone you love,' she said, 'and have far-reaching consequences.' It could only mean that Mrs Hepher is going to tell me that Wilhelmina has the makings of a prime minister. Hm! There's nothing new that anybody can tell me about Miss Bossy Boots. To cheer me up, however, the gypsy promised, 'You will succeed in your goals – if you learn to distinguish enemies from friends.'

The salon was the busiest it's ever been. I was rushed

131

off my feet from opening time at nine o'clock until I saw the last customer out the door at ten past five.

I'm so angry about that carpenter! Twice I rang him and got his answer-phone. It's very embarrassing when customers sit down to wait their turn. Every time I looked up, there they all were, leaning at a thirty-degree angle and squashed up to each other for support. It was the one at the bottom end I felt sorry for. Fancy having the weight of eight heavy bodies piled up against you. It was very gallant of Grandad Pitts to volunteer for that position. 'I hope you're not driven by no ulterior motive!' Maggie declared, and was quite taken aback when he retaliated, 'Give o'er, woman! I 'ad them tekken out *years* ago!'

We did hear some interesting conversations, though. One of the women from Rosamund Street commented on Sonya's possible forthcoming operation, adding for Bertha Twistle's benefit, 'You know old Bill Bent as used to keep the cobbler's on Tanner Street?'

'Aye,' replied Bertha, taking her life in her hands and leaning forward – sideways, 'I know the feller.'

'Well, his wife . . . Gladys . . . she's just had the very same operation as Sonya might have.'

'What? Yer mean . . .?'

'Aye! Women's trouble. 'Isterectomy . . . the very same. Not a nice business, is it, eh?'

'What's that?' Fred Twistle didn't like to be left out of any conversation, especially when he could see everyone so interested. Cupping his hand behind his deaf ear, he repeated the question to his roly-poly wife. 'What's that yer say, Bertha?'

'You remember old Bill the cobbler?'

'Ol' Bill? Aye.' He strained his ears so as not to miss a word.

'Well, Gladys, Bill's wife, she's 'ad 'isterectomy.'

'Gerraway!' Fred was flabbergasted. 'Ol' Bill's never 'ad erectomy! The feller must be bloody eighty if 'e's a day. Naw! I'm tellin' you, Bertha Twistle, if *I* can't erectomy I'm damned sure ol' Bill the cobbler can't!'

'Ooh, yer a silly ol' fool, Fred Twistle!' Bertha was embarrassed by the roar of laughter which erupted from every corner. 'It's Bill's *wife* . . . *Gladys*! She's 'ad 'er womb tekken out, yer gormless ancient!'

'Eh?' The penny appeared to drop. 'Oh, well, at least they'll not be 'avin' any more childer, then.'

At this point, the exasperated Bertha got up to have her hair trimmed, leaving everybody to slide down a place and Dora Leadbeater from Rosamund Street to continue the conversation. 'Don't be daft, man! Gladys Bent's sixty-eight!'

'Six to eight!' Fred Twistle could hardly believe his ears. 'By! There's carelessness fer yer! That's enough bloody childer fer anybody to cope with. It's comin' ter some'at when the buggers ain't sure whether they've got six or eight! If yer ask me, it's just as well 'e can't 'ave erectomy . . . that's what I say!' And having said it, he began whistling 'Underneath the lamplight' and fell on top of the woman from the tripe shop.

Thursday, October 1st

It's been one of those days again. A man turned up at half past ten this morning to fit a telephone extension in the salon. It was absolute chaos! There were cables everywhere, and we were so busy that no matter which way he turned the man was trampling on, or tripping over, somebody. There wasn't enough room to swing a cat. He didn't take offence, though, when he got a short

133

back and sides he hadn't asked for. What he did object to was having his doojemeflop clutched by Granny Grabber every time he bent down. The poor thing was fair hobbling when he left. He must have told a few pals who didn't mind that sort of thing, because three of them turned up one after the other to check the line. They all left with smiles on their faces. And Granny Grabber thought it was her birthday! I wouldn't mind, but she'd only stopped by to pass the time of day. She has made a solid booking now, though – to have the whiskers taken off her top lip.

At lunch time I had a stinking row with that skiving carpenter! 'I'll be out as soon as ever I can, missus,' he told me, in unnecessarily harsh tones. I reminded him that he'd had quite long enough to come back and rectify his mistake. I also made the point that poor Larkin found herself perched on the high end of the seat this morning, and her little legs couldn't even reach the floor.

'She was absolutely terrified,' I said, 'all that way up in the air with her legs dangling. She became quite dizzy.' I didn't tell him that when she reached such a pitch of nervousness the inevitable happened. Thinking it was an earthquake, everybody ran out into the street. It took me ages to round them up again, by which time little Larkin (having lost the support of her neighbours) had slid to the bottom of the seat, toppled off the edge and knocked herself clean out. 'I insist that you get out here and do the job,' I told the fellow. He said he'd do his best to get out first thing in the morning.

I had to call the doctor out, as both Tom and Wilhelmina were bright pink at breakfast time. I thought they'd been up to something until Tom turned green at the sight of his egg and Wilhelmina didn't answer back when

Maggie called her a warmonger. They've both got measles, and are confined to bed. Maggie says she hopes to catch them, so that 'my Ethelbert will be able to nurse me'. (It takes all sorts.)

I'd no sooner shut the salon for the day than Sonya rang from the infirmary. 'Come and get me, gal!' she said. 'Get yersel' a taxi, an' I'll see yer right.'

When I got there, she was sitting at the bottom of the steps outside the front entrance. 'Miserable bloody place!' she muttered, clambering into the taxi. It was then that I noticed her black eye. 'Don't ask,' she said, ''cause yer'll only say it serves me right.'

'I won't,' I promised. And when she told me how she got it, I kept my promise. And I did not laugh! (At least, not until I was in the privacy of my own parlour, where I related the tale to Maggie, in fits of hysterics. Maggie roared. 'Serves her right!' she said. And it did!)

It seems that, once the doctor had told her there was no need for a hysterectomy, and that her condition was due to malabsorption in her digestive system (easily treated by diet), Sonya felt the need to celebrate her reinstated femininity. Having already found that one of her old clients was working as groundsman there, she slipped him a note. The consequence was that, at midnight, Sonya and another frustrated patient by the name of Rosa (who had been undergoing treatment for her varicose veins) rearranged their bedclothes so they wouldn't be missed, and crept away to meet two blokes in the gardener's tool-shed. 'I tell yer, gal, I ain't never seen a set o' tools like 'em! Well, I told Rosa, I said, them buggers 'ave been looked after right well, that clean and shiny they were. In my opinion, they shoulda been bloody well framed!'

The upshot of all this creeping about at midnight came

some half-hour later, when the ward-sister realized there were two patients missing. Help was recruited, and an all-out search undertaken, inevitably spilling out into the grounds. 'Frightened the arse off me,' Sonya said, 'all these bloody torch-lights and charging figures! I ain't kiddin' yer, gal! I thought, "Christ! The ol' feller's right . . . the buggers 'ave invaded!"'

In the ensuing panic, Rosa and her fellow shot out of the shed and, stark naked and terrified, fled into the chapel, where, after coming cheek by jowl with two departed souls stretched out in their last sleep, they meekly (and thankfully) surrendered. Back in the shed, the groundsman had gone on his knees, pleading with Sonya to say it was all her fault, and that he had tried to dissuade her. 'It's me job, y'see,' he'd told her, 'I don't want ter lose me job.'

Sonya was not impressed, and told him so. 'Tipped a bag o' fertilizer o'er 'im, I did!' she said, obviously disgusted at such cowardice. Then she stood tall, straightened her shoulders, and decided to emerge from the shed with honour. The effect was somewhat marred, however, when she stepped on an upturned rake, which swung up and smacked her in the eye.

'Can't you even go into hospital for a couple of days without getting desperate for a man?' I asked her.

'Nope!' she replied. So I left it at that.

Friday, October 2nd

Sonya came into work today as though nothing had happened. Her black eye had turned a spectacular technicolour. 'Come on, gal!' she laughed. 'Let's 'ave the mop-'eads in!'

Maggie was kept busy with the children, rushing up and down stairs with Ethelbert bringing up the rear. 'Isn't this exciting?' he was heard to remark. When I went in at lunch time, he was flaked out in the armchair, purple and breathless. It's not *my* business to ask what they'd been up to.

'He will overdo it!' Maggie complained, quite put out. 'I've told him he's not as young as he'd like to think!' (She's no piglet herself, is she?)

You know, something really ought to be done about Mad Aggie. She went past the window twice today, doing cartwheels. I was trimming Ted Dewsbury's bushy eyebrows at the time. I'm afraid the sudden appearance of that mountainous pink bulge quite unnerved me. Now the poor fellow's walking about with no eyebrows at all, and a permanently startled expression.

Saturday, October 3rd

I think that brunette must have moved in with Barny Singleton. She was at the window in her dressing-gown this morning (the brazen hussy). And when she caught me looking, she had the nerve to wave. They deserve each other.

Smelly Kelly booked an appointment this morning (thank God he *rang*). I've booked him in at five thirty on Monday, when everybody else has gone. That'll give me a chance to fumigate the place before the following morning.

The damned carpenter didn't turn up again. I left a message on his answer-phone to tell him that if he hadn't repaired the bench by Monday evening I was getting someone else in – and sending the bill to him.

There's been nothing but trouble on that telephone line since we had the extension fitted. I'd been trying all morning to get through to Tiffany (thought it was time I checked up on her). And there were all sort of noises going on – crackling, and people talking. This afternoon, when I tried yet again, Sonya was there. She could see the state I was getting in. 'Fer Gawd's sake, give it 'ere!' she ordered. She told me to get on the extension and she'd show me how it was done. 'Patience!' she said. 'Yer must 'ave patience!'

When she dialled the number, a woman's voice said, 'All the lines are engaged.'

'Piss orf!' Sonya shrieked, slamming the phone down. When I reminded her that she was supposed to exercise patience, she looked at me with her technicolour eye and laughed. 'Yer quite right, Jessica, gal . . . an' so I shall.' We picked up the phones once more, and she carefully dialled Tiffany's number again, smiling at me smugly while she waited for someone to answer.

Presently a man's voice came on the line, and then a woman's, all lovey dovey and cooing at each other. I'm ashamed to say that both Sonya and I listened pop-eyed as they went over every detail of their encounter the night before. 'And do you still love me, Nathan darling?' asked the woman. We all waited breathlessly.

'Of course I do, heaven-sent,' came the reply. They then moved on to describe and praise parts of each other's anatomy that I never knew existed! And oh, the positions! Well, I couldn't do that, even if Barny Singleton gave me the opportunity . . . I've got my perforated ear-drum to think of. Their revelations and obvious desire for each other were proving increasingly embarrassing, although I thought it wonderful that two people could be so devoted to each other. Covering up my mouthpiece, I whispered to Sonya to put the phone down, and we'd try again.

'Not bloody likely!' she retorted. 'Keep doin' that an' yer'll never get through! I'll shift this pair off, you see if I don't!' I thought she was about to employ a barrage of colourful language, but instead she waited for a break in the conversation (during which there was much moaning and sighing) and said, mimicking the woman's voice, 'I know you think you're God's gift to women, Nathan, but I wish you'd do something about your bad breath. It quite sickens me!'

There was a gasp from both sides, then a shocked silence before Nathan's voice rang out, 'You bitch! And what about you, eh? What about that awful dog-shit you call perfume? Talk about a turn-off!' There followed a tearful noise before the phone was slammed down.

'There y'are, gal!' chuckled Sonya. 'Nowt to it!'

She got me through to Tiffany, who (I was delighted to hear) was not going to kill herself after all. 'I'm going to kill them instead!' she said.

It was one of those days when you wished you'd stayed in bed.

Monday, October 5th

The carpenter turned up at five fifteen, just as Flo Tewkes was leaving. 'There's no need to be so nasty!' he said, slamming about. 'I do my best.' I thought he was about to start crying. 'It never seems good enough, though! You do a job, and the minute your back's turned folks start complaining, pulling your work to pieces and calling you back again for the slightest thing. You've no idea!' I think he must have got out on the wrong side of the bed. 'And I'm not at all well,' he mumbled, gripping his hands round his middle and burping. 'Do pardon me – my stomach's playing funny tricks.' He proceeded to prise the bench from the floor.

'Do be careful,' I pleaded, seeing the floorboards begin to lift.

'There you are!' He raised his brows in a helpless gesture. That's exactly what I mean . . . you women are all the same. You will not let me get on with the job. I do know what I'm doing, you know!' It was most unfortunate that as he bent down to resume his work two things happened simultaneously. Little Larkin's face appeared at the window, and as she strained up to ask if I could set her hair on Wednesday, there was a distinct clap of thunder. At the same instant, Smelly Kelly walked in and overpowered us all.

'Oh my goodness!' stuttered the carpenter, straightening up to clutch his stomach. 'I have to go!' and he legged it away up the road, leaving his work-bag behind. I left a message on his answer-phone telling him that if he didn't get back on the job I would dispose of his tools. That should do it.

The children are looking better. Lucky's brought a Great Dane home and he's been strutting about all day, showing her round. From the arrogant look on his face, he obviously thinks he's in charge. I can just hear him telling his new friend how difficult we are to control.

Sonya's eye is much calmer, and not quite so painful. She told me earlier that it was just as well, because she's got roaring Ronald coming round at midnight. 'What does he do?' I foolishly asked.

'Not a lot,' she replied, ''E thinks 'e's Ronald Reagan. 'E sort o' pokes 'is nose where it's no right ter be. Then we do a cowboy scene . . . lots o' lassooin' an' rump-brandin'.'

'Where! Camp David?'

'Oh no! *E*'s away on a fortnight's 'oliday!'

(There's no one to blame but myself.)

There's to be a meeting in the Memorial Hall at seven thirty on Thursday night. It's for all the Casey Court women (so nice to feel at home at last) and it's to do with Smelly Kelly. 'You go, Jessica,' Maggie suggested, 'I'll stay here with my Ethelbert and the children.' According to Sonya, Smelly Kelly's going to 'get 'is come-uppance'. I don't really want to go either.

There's a knicker-pincher on the loose. There have been several frilly sets taken from various washing-lines. The only ones that were left untouched were Big Barbara's from No. 19. Sonya wasn't surprised, though. 'I expect 'e thought they were barrage balloons left over from the war,' she snorted. Apparently, Sonya and Big Barbara are old enemies. Big Barbara got to hear what Sonya said, and has issued a challenge. It's no holds barred and a fight to the death, outside Charlie's Chip-shop at midnight on Saturday.

Sonya says she'll 'mek bloody mincemeat out on 'er'. Big Barbara sent a message back saying not before Sonya ends up in Charlie's chipper, she won't. Maggie says it's just like 'Gunfight on the Old Corral', and Tom has declared he's on Barbara's side. Wilhelmina informed us that she was 'above that sort of thing'. Our Ethelbert is selling grandstand tickets at 50p each, the 'grandstand' being Fred Twistle's pigeon-loft. They're splitting the profits between them.

It says in the local paper that Singleton's Barber-shop is going unisex and that there will be a free ladies' day on Tuesday of next week. The first fifteen newcomers would be 'serviced' free of charge. It sounds like a stud-farm. But then, that's Barny Singleton's style, I shouldn't wonder.

'He's declaring war!' said Maggie, and promptly put on her tin hat.

Sonya was more colourful. 'Why, the schemin' bugger!' she shrieked. ''E's out ter *flatten* yer!' Chance would be a fine thing!

'I'm not bothered,' I lied. He can try every trick in the book, but he'll not get the better of me!

When I was checking the bookings this evening, I found that Fred Twistle's head-shave hadn't been confirmed for tomorrow. It wasn't like Fred, because he was so proud of his shiny bald head, and never missed an appointment.

The children had been fed. I had dutifully dabbed them all over with camomile lotion, and as they appeared to be sleeping I asked Maggie whether she'd mind me popping down the road to see whether Fred still wanted the appointment. 'Not at all,' she said, as I knew she would, 'you go and see what's ailing him.'

I passed Granny Grabber, who was busy washing her front doorstep. ''Ow do, Mrs Jolly,' she called out, slapping a wet hand up my skirt and squeezing my prime parts. 'Lovely evening, ain't it?'

'It certainly is,' I smiled. It's not easy to smile when your wet thighs cause you to walk with one leg here and one in Texas.

It was Bertha Twistle who answered the door, looking flushed and breathless. 'I've come to see whether Fred

142

still wants his appointment first thing,' I said. 'If he doesn't I can pop into town to get some supplies . . . the rep's let me down again.'

'Well, you'd best go through an' ask 'im yersel', Mrs Jolly,' she retorted. 'The bugger ain't speakin' ter me, is 'e?' With that, she dragged me in and slammed the door. I knew straight away that I'd walked into a family row, and I felt very uncomfortable. 'Go on through!' she said, waddling behind me and giving me the occasional push. 'Yer just the one ter settle an argument . . . being neutered an' all that!' (I didn't know it showed.)

'Really, Bertha,' I protested, 'I don't think it's my place to get involved.'

'Away with yer! Ye've only to tell 'im that what I'm saying makes sense,' she urged.

Apparently two of Fred's pigeons had gone missing. 'All as I found i' the birds' loft this morning were 'andful o' feathers an' a bloody gurt 'ole i' the wire mesh. That were one of 'er mangy moggies!' he exploded, stamping about the room and shaking his fist.

'It ain't!' protested Bertha, growing pinker by the minute. 'My darlin's wouldn't eat one o' your bloody birds . . . not even if they were starvin' they wouldn't!'

'I'll strangle every last one o' the buggers!' came the reply. 'You see if I don't!'

I didn't wait to see. Once I'd managed to establish that he was keeping his appointment, I was off. When forced to give an opinion, though, I made the best offering I could. 'It's the knicker-pincher,' I said, and left them to it.

Ethelbert told Maggie that it might be a good idea to get the chimney swept before the winter comes. Old Pops never did, and 'the soot up there must be coated four inches or more'. So I phoned 'Abe Sweep – who does it on the cheap' (I wonder if he's one of Sonya's?). 'Oi'll be oot the morrer,' he said, in a west country drawl. I'm glad I'm not the only foreigner. He rang back later to ask whether it would be all right to sweep the chimney on Friday instead; 'Oi've lorst me boike, d'ye see?'

'Of course that's all right,' I told him. Well, what else could I say? I mean, how can he clean my chimney without his bike?

Wednesday, October 7th

The salon was buzzing with talk of an article that appeared in the local paper this morning. 'They're sayin' as 'ow it don't seem logical to leave Casey's Court standin' when they've pulled everythin' down around it,' reported her from Rosamund Street, 'an' ter tell yer the truth, I can see their point!'

'That's 'cause you don't live in Casey's Court!' accused Marny Tupp, from the Barge Inn. 'I've kept yon pub at the corner 'ere for nigh on twenty year, an' I'll tell yer this! If they pull down Casey's Court, they'll do it over my dead body, an' that's a fact!' He meant it, too.

'An' don't think the buggers wouldn't,' piped in Sonya, stepping back to admire her client's quiff. 'We daren't none of us turn us backs fer too long, else they'll 'ave them bulldozers in an' reduce us to rubble afore yer can say where's it gone?'

Little Larkin burst into tears. 'They mustn't be allowed to do it,' she sobbed, 'they mustn't!'

'Don't you worry, sweet'eart!' Sonya went over and gave her a bear-hug. 'Just let the sods try it, that's all. I'm a match fer any o' them bulldozers. They'll not get past me, I'm tellin' yer!' There came a volley of support from one and all, in the midst of which the brick I'd put under one end of the bench collapsed in a heap. Eight bodies collapsed in a bigger one.

'Gawd Almighty!' shouted Nora Denton, who'd been quietly doing her knitting. 'I've lost all me stitches!'

In the confusion, somebody misheard, thinking Nora Denton had lost all her breeches. It was enough to take their minds off their bruises and get them started on the subject of the knicker-pincher, who was still at large.

When I finally locked the salon door, I felt mentally and physically exhausted.

'Just look at that!' Sonya said, seeing Barny Singleton helping the brunette out of his car. 'You'd think 'e'd learnt 'is lesson, wouldn't yer, eh?'

'She's very attractive, though,' I said, feeling small inside. 'Who is she, Sonya?'

'Don't yer know, gal?' She seemed astonished. 'That's Gloria . . . 'is wife as was! It looks like she's back in favour!' (And here I am, head over heels in love with him.)

Thursday, October 8th

I'll have to arrange for the rep to call after closing hours in future. It's too embarrassing discussing my order in front of the customers. There were no problems with the shampoo and other hair paraphernalia – it was when he came to replenish the condom stock that uproar reigned. He was inundated from all sides with lewd and unnecessary comments. There was no need whatsoever for Fred Twistle to give a graphic and horrifying account of his prowess as a lad. 'It's a pity we didn't have a choice in those days,' he said. 'It were a rubber macintosh an' wellies, never mind pink, see-through an' extra-long . . . yer got what yer were given, whether it strangled yer or

145

not!' I don't know if I'll ever get used to such outright behaviour, I really don't.

I was so tired after I'd helped Maggie wash up and get the children comfortable that I fell fast asleep in the armchair. It was eleven o'clock when I was woken up by Maggie. 'Come on,' she said, 'you'd best get yourself off to bed, or you'll be fit for nothing in the morning.'

I was horrified that I'd slept for so long. 'Oh, Maggie!' I said, remembering. 'I was supposed to go to that meeting about Smelly Kelly! Whatever will Sonya think?'

'She came by to collect you about eight o'clock, and when she saw you asleep she said you were not to be bothered, and she'd tell you all about it in the morning.' With a smile, she added, 'You've got a good friend there, my girl . . . for all her peculiarities.'

'I know,' I agreed, taking Maggie's hand and squeezing it, 'and I've got a good friend in you, as well.' After I'd looked in on the children (spots gone, but still somewhat flushed) I climbed into bed to make these notes in my diary. I feel more contented that I've been for a long time. I can't stop thinking about Barny Singleton, however much I try. I know it's wrong, and I should be glad for his son's sake that he and his wife are reconciled. But somehow it makes little difference to the way I feel about him. Even if he can never be mine, and even though he wants to put me out of business, I love him – and I hate him!

Friday, October 9th

I'm pleased to say that the carpenter returned. I now have a level bench. The chimney sweep proved to be a far greater trial. He meticulously covered everything over, and when he'd secured the cloth over the fireplace, he pushed the brush up the flap and told Maggie, 'Goo out the back dooer an' watch fer this 'ere brush to pop out the top o' the chimney,' which she did. She watched for ages but it never appeared. There went on a long and noisy exchange, in which he would shout to her and she would shout to him, and both would wave their arms. After a while, it got a little heated when Maggie began to jump up and down, and the sweep lost his temper. 'Now look 'ere, m'dear,' he mouthed through the window. 'Ye ain't tellin' me as ye can't see it yet?' He began ramming it up and down until the roof was seen to tremble. Of a sudden there came a splitting, roaring sound.

'It's coming! I can hear it now,' shouted Maggie, at which point the brush came whizzing out of the chimney, bearing aloft a spherical object with knobs on. 'Whatever is it?' Maggie asked Ethelbert, who had come to investigate what his sweetheart was getting so worked up about. Before he could answer, the sweep withdrew his brush, and the round thing began to roll down the roof.

'Bloody Nora!' yelled Ethelbert. 'It's a bomb!' He grabbed hold of Maggie, lost his balance in the panic, and the two of them ended up in her bunker – with the spiked metal ball resting precariously on the edge!

It later turned out to be a battered money-box into which old Pops had hammered long jagged nails, possibly to deter would-be thieves. It contained one hundred and fifty pounds and a rolled up photograph of Marilyn Monroe, with a painted on moustache. 'He never could stand 'em perfect,' explained Ethelbert.

Maggie and Ethelbert are more in love than ever. He's very proud of himself, strutting about and telling everybody he always knew he had nerves of steel. Maggie's annoyed that, just when she needed it most, she was caught without her tin hat!

When the excitement had died down, Sonya told me that there had been a unanimous decision at the meeting last night. 'That Kelly's been without a bath so long,' she said, 'there's dirt on his dirt, his clothes are stiff, an' it's time 'e were dunked in a tub o' water!' A plan had been devised to lure him into Sonya's parlour, where there'd be waiting a tin bath full of hot soapy water, and half a dozen volunteers to strip him off. 'Are yer game, gal?' she asked me.

'I'd rather not,' I told her. 'I don't know him very well.'

'Now's yer chance,' she said, slapping me on the back. 'Ye'll know the bugger as well as any on us after Sunday night!' And before I could think of a good enough reason to refuse, she'd gone.

'You go and give the women a hand!' Maggie said. 'You're young and strong. And anyway, it'll be nice not to have your shop emptied every time he walks in!' That was true enough.

Tom and Wilhelmina look almost normal now. 'I won't have to go back to school on Monday, will I?' asked Wilhelmina. It gave me great pleasure to tell her that she would.

Saturday, October 10th

I spent all morning trying to talk Sonya out of meeting Big Barbara outside Charlie's Chip-shop tonight. It really worries me. 'Do me a favour, gal,' she chortled, 'I'll wipe the floor wi' the ol' bag! It'll be over in minutes, you'll see!' She would not be deterred. And those who had bought grandstand tickets also shouted me down.

148

'Give over!' Ethelbert argued. ''Ow else can yer settle some'at like this? I don't know the way they do things down south, but this is meat-an'-tatty-pie country, an' we've allus settled us differences in an 'onourable fashion!' Then he sold four more tickets. Maggie was ever so proud of him.

'You could run the Stock Exchange,' she said.

Sonya was right, though. It was all over in minutes. Big Barbara slung a fist and caved in Charlie's Chip-shop window, Sonya dived at her and ripped off her blouse, and Granny Grabber got too close and was knocked clean out. A roar went up from Fred Twistle's pigeon-loft, then loud screams as the whole thing collapsed like a pack of cards, releasing dozens of terrified pigeons to drop bombs everywhere. And, in the midst of chaos, the police arrived and arrested everybody.

At three o'clock this morning we were all released, after promising to keep the peace. I was confronted by my favourite bobby. 'You again! I shall make a special note of this,' he said, licking his pen and scribbling things into his pad. He's becoming a real irritant. It's a good job Maggie stayed in to mind the children. It's also a good job he doesn't know that I'm to take part in the stripping and force-bathing of a twenty-stone male tomorrow night!

Sunday, October 11th

I don't know how I shall ever be able to look myself in the face again! I'll certainly never be able to look Smelly Kelly in the face again (at least, not without certain terrifying images of huge dimensions looming up before me, as well as other embarrassing recollections, not so terrifying but best forgotten nevertheless).

Never having been inundated with offers from the female of the species (since he took their breath away so they couldn't speak – couldn't breathe either, I shouldn't wonder) poor Smelly Kelly thought all his birthdays had arrived at the same time when Sonya shoved a note through his door. 'I'm feeling lonely,' it said. 'If you're not doing anything about eight o'clock tonight, perhaps you'd make your way down to No. 4. I'm sure you'll be pleasantly surprised.'

He was surprised right enough! The poor chap had no sooner poked his nose in the parlour than they were on him. In the time it takes to peel a banana they had him starkers, roaring and fighting like a mad bull and flailing his arms about at anything that moved. Sonya got quite excited. ''Old the bugger down!' she yelled above the din. 'Shove 'im under, warts an' all!' There was an undignified scuffle, a shout of 'Gerroff me soddin' foot!' And a kind of wet frantic gurgle. The last thing I saw before Sonya shouted 'Jessica, don't just stand there! Fotch the car-bolic!' was a thrashing mountain of wet hairy flesh, a pair of startled black eyes and a thick bushy beard covered in soap which all in a minute had disappeared beneath the frothing water. As he went in, a tidal wave swept out and swamped us all; then, as everybody surged forward to keep him down while he was frantically scrubbed, some-body knocked my arm and the soap shot out of my fingers. It lurched into the air and fell with a plop into the tin bath. 'Grab the bugger!' screamed Sonya. Caught up in the mood of the moment, I plunged my arm beneath the suds and groped about. For the life of me, I don't know how it happened, but without warning Kelly gave out a fearful roar and rose up like the demon from the black lagoon. Swinging first this way, then that, he sent all six of us in different directions. I don't know what he swung at the woman from the tripe shop, but she ended up wedged tight between the telly and the sideboard. Milly Channer went up that passage and out of the front door like greased lightning, and Bertha Twistle spun round like a top and fell over cross-eyed. The rest of us were scattered like ninepins.

'I'll kill the lot of yer!' roared Kelly, stepping out of the bath in all his glory.

'Ooha!' cooed Sonya, looking him up and down. He really was strikingly handsome – a bit like James Robertson Justice, only younger. He was certainly well-endowed – at least, there were parts of him that still dangled in the water when they had no call to.

'I'm going home,' I told Sonya. 'I'll send Ethelbert straight back.' (I admit it – I'm a coward.)

'Oh no,' she said, 'don't do that.' She had her eye fixed on that towering torso of manhood, and she was quite mesmerized. 'Keep the ol' feller there a while longer.'

When the rest of us drowned rats hurriedly took our leave, it suddenly struck me at the door that Kelly might be too much of a handful for Sonya, and she was my friend, after all. So I went back, with the intention of offering whatever help I could. I won't reveal what I saw in that parlour, but suffice it to say that when I looked in the door our Sonya had everything under control. Well – almost everything.

When I got home, the children were in bed, and Maggie was having a meal with Ethelbert. I crept past, locked the scullery door, had a swift wash, and called it a night.

I ache from top to bottom.

Sonya and Kelly are engaged! 'I'm giving up all my other
fellers,' she said, at half past ten this morning, ''cause I'm
in love.' (I've heard it all before.) At nine o'clock this
evening she came round, slammed herself into the chair
and moaned, 'Soddin' fellers! They think they own yer!' I
think that probably means that she and Kelly are finished.
'Let's tek up jogging,' she said. 'I'm gerrin' a bit thick
round me arse!'

'All right,' I agreed (because I am as well). We're going
to town tomorrow afternoon (all my P.M. women have
cancelled to take advantage of Barny Singleton's free
'service') and we're getting properly geared up. We'll start
jogging at seven A.M. on Wednesday morning.

'I'll bet yer don't mek it as far as Fiona's Flower-shop!'
challenged Sonya.

'I bet I will!' I replied (and I will . . . even if it kills
me).

Wilhelmina went to school as quiet as a lamb – it
worries me. Freckle-faced Winnie came for her at quarter
to nine. 'I'm going to school as well!' she said, proud as a
peacock – that worried me more. I told Maggie to make
sure that Wilhelmina went right inside the door.

When she came back, she said she'd watched the pair
of them disappear into the school along with a crowd of
other children. 'Perhaps she's getting to like school at
last?' she suggested, hoping to allay my fears. I must have
a naturally suspicious nature, because I'm still not happy
about it – I must remember to have a word with Mrs
Hepher.

Tom was a real pain this morning. First he was throwing
tantrums, then he went into a dark and dirty sulk. Thank
God for Maggie and Ethelbert! They cajoled Tom into a

game of snap and let him beat them three times. That cheered him up no end – so much so that he threw his arms round Lucky's neck and swung him about. Lucky wasn't too pleased, being in a deep sleep at the time. In fact it gave him a terrible fright, and he clamped his teeth into Tom's foot and wouldn't let go, until Maggie had the good sense to offer him a piece of the beef I'd prepared for tonight's salad. Tom's foot's all right, just slightly bruised. But he'll need a new pair of socks. Maggie says these things are sent to try us. (I say it's Tom who's sent to try us.)

Ethelbert's got a secret! Maggie says he's been acting very strangely – saying things like 'Would you rather stroke something smooth, or something hairy?' and 'Is there anything about me that you'd change if you could?' When she told him to stop being silly, and that she adored him just as he was, he told her that before too long she'd be 'in for a great surprise'. She's been trembling with anticipation all evening. I've warned her that she and her Ethelbert are at the time of life when surprises can do more harm than good. I've also pointed out that it's never a good idea to keep secrets from each other. She reacted in a very peculiar manner, putting her arm round me and asking in a fearful voice, 'Would you ever forgive me if you found out I was keeping secrets from you?' I told her that of course I would, and that I loved her. As mother-in-laws go, she must be one of the best.

'I'd probably forgive you anything,' I said, adding: 'Anyway . . . what possible secrets could we have from each other? We live in each other's pockets!' She gave no reply, but went very quiet and pale. I expect she's at that funny time of life. And then there's Ethelbert, sending up her blood pressure every chance he gets (randy old sod.

I've seen him, nibbling her ear and running his tobacco-stained fingers over her prominent parts).

They're back! The marathon bonkers must have crept in some time in the night, because I never heard a thing until four o'clock this morning, when the whole house was gyrating on its foundations. Tom grabbed his Lego-land, Wilhelmina grabbed Tom, and the pair of them rushed into my and Maggie's room, wide-eyed and clutching each other. Maggie shot up in bed, looking fearsome in new psychedelic pink rollers and bright green face-pack. 'Is there an earthquake or what?' she shouted above the noise.

'Oh, I know what it is!' said Wilhelmina, obviously relieved. 'It's those two next door. They're at it again.'

Once that was established, we all tried to get back to sleep, which wasn't easy with the earth shaking beneath us. 'I'll report them to the Council!' threatened Maggie. She won't. Not when she comes round to thinking about her Ethelbert – she's not the envying sort, isn't Maggie.

We were busy in the salon today. It was mostly men, and a rush of mothers bringing their little lads in straight after school. We had one customer who came along without an appointment, and insisted on Sonya doing it. It was Kelly. Not smelly any more, and looking quite presentable in a tweed flap-back jacket and green cords. 'Are you going 'unting or some'at?' asked Sonya, with a touch of sarcasm. When he told her that the only thing he had in mind to hunt was her, she went all silly and flushed. 'Gerraway, you daft thing!' she said, pushing him on the shoulder. By the time she'd finished trimming his beard, they'd fixed up a date for Saturday night.

'You just watch him!' warned Bertha Twistle from beneath the hair-dryer. ''E's a big feller, is yon!' I wonder if I was the only one to see Sonya's eyes light up.

154

'Ain't 'e gorgeous, now 'e's clean an' shiny?' she asked me, and I had to admit he was a strikingly handsome lump. 'D'yer know who 'e reminds me of?'

'No,' I said.

'That feller in that coal advert on the telly . . . y'know the one? 'E wears a kilt an' warms 'is arse afront o' the telly . . . waggles it side to side wi' the music!' Then she went into a daydream and squirted a whole tube of shaving-cream up Mrs Flannagan's nose.

Tiffany wants to come and stay for a week. Maggie was horrified. 'We don't want strangers here,' she said. (Fancy that! Maggie's usually quite sociable.)

Tuesday, October 13th

In view of Maggie's seeming horror of having Tiffany here, I've suggested she might like to go on holiday that week. 'I'm not being shoved off for this Tiffany's convenience!' she snorted.

That bloody Barny Singleton! (Forgive me, Lord, for swearing.) But we only had one customer in this morning – and that was only Mad Aggie wanting her toe-nails trimmed. Sonya told her to 'piss orf to the vet's', which must have struck her on a funny bone, because she left in fits of laughter, doing cartwheels all down the road.

It became obvious that we weren't going to get much custom for the day, so I told Sonya she could go home and I'd see her about twelve o'clock. It was at that point that Ethelbert strolled in. 'Is my sweetheart in the parlour?' he asked, looking every bit like the cat who'd had the cream. Intrigued by his manner, Sonya and I followed him through. We watched from the door while he manoeuvred Maggie into a chair, telling her in an authoritative voice, 'Prepare yourself, Maggie Flaherty! You're about to see something you'll never forget!' Then he whipped off his cap and stepped forward a pace.

'Oh, my Gawd!' gasped Sonya. 'The daft bugger's killed one o' Bertha Twistle's moggies!' For a minute there, I thought the same.

Tom took one look at the black hairy thing draped over Ethelbert's head and ran behind Maggie. Lucky growled at it, and Sonya and I crept back into the salon, where we doubled up in fits of laughter. Maggie loved it, though. 'You look just like Clark Gable,' she said, and threw herself into his arms (we heard the crash as the pair of them fell over against the sideboard).

What a time Sonya and I had round the shops! We went into the Co-op and tried on all the hats; Sonya favoured a red pill-box with a cheeky little veil, and I fell overboard for a sexy black trilby with a yellow rose in the brim. We were having a great time, eyeing ourselves this way and that in the mirror, until a frosty-faced store-woman came up and ushered us away. 'It's obvious you have no intention of buying,' she said, snatching the hats away and replacing them. Sonya gave the woman a rather vulgar V sign (I wasn't at all surprised when the manager was sent for and we were escorted off the premises).

There was a sale on at one big store, and we sauntered about picking up armfuls of skirts and dresses which we took to the fitting rooms and tried on. It was hot in those little cubicles, and the smell of those who had gone before clung in the air like choking vapour. I could actually *taste* cheap heady perfume. I felt dangerously claustrophobic, having to rush out from behind the curtains three times. When Sonya saw me gasping for air, she said, 'My cubicle's just the same . . . I reckon little Larkin's about!' Everything hung on me like a sack, and the vivid colours made me look like a sick parrot. 'Yer too bloody skinny, Jessica Jolly!' declared Sonya. 'I dunno about jogging . . . yer should be eating a dozen cream-cakes a day!' Talking of jogging, I reminded her that it was track-suits we'd come to buy. 'Yer right!' she agreed, holding up a blue and white spotted mini-dress, with Al Capone shoulders, priced at eighteen pounds, and a pair of scarlet skin-tight trousers priced at twenty-six pounds. 'Now then – which d'yer think?' When I told her I wasn't particularly struck by the dress she conceded, 'Naw . . . it ain't me, is it? I'm partial to these 'ere trousers, though.' Whereupon she skilfully and shamelessly switched the price tickets.

'Hey! You can't do that!' I protested.

'I bloody can,' she said. '*I'm 'avin these trousers!*' And she would have done, if I hadn't wrestled both articles from her, after a real struggle (it's a good job I was able to camouflage that jagged tear in the mini-dress that went from collar to hem), in the ensuing fight.

'Any good?' asked the assistant as I boldly handed them back. I shook my head and thanked her all the same.

Sonya, however, was still in a fit of pique with me. 'I should check that frock,' she told the girl. 'My friend 'ere's a bit of a rough 'un when she's tryin' things on.' When the puzzled girl looked me up and down my face went every shade of scarlet. And when, a suspicious look growing on her face, she began examining the garments, I hastened my steps, while trying to appear casual and unruffled. Once outside, I took off up the street as if the devil was after me – as it was, in the shape of Sonya. 'Hey! Wait for me!' she yelled, falling about on her four-inch stilettoes. 'Else if the buggers catch me I'll tell 'em yer known as the phantom frock-ripper! They'll put yer

157

away fer bloody years!' With friends like her, who needs enemies?

There was a worse palaver in the sports shop. First of all, Sonya couldn't decide between a plum-coloured track-suit with a yellow stripe down each leg and an orange one with nauseating green flowers all over it. 'I'll try 'em both,' she said, and asked to be pointed in the direction of the fitting rooms.

'Oh, we don't have fitting rooms,' the man replied, his blue eyes popping and the vein in his temple throbbing visibly (I couldn't take my eyes off it).

'No bloody fittin' rooms?' Sonya moaned. 'Where the 'ell am I supposed ter try these track-suits on? If yer think I'm cockin' my arse up afront of everybody ye've gorranother think comin'.'

This tickled one young fellow, who told his mates with a wink, 'We wouldn't mind seeing a middle-aged wrinkly arse, would we, eh?' The smile slipped from his face, to be replaced by a definitely cross-eyed expression, when Sonya fetched him one with her handbag.

'My bloody arse *ain't* wrinkled,' she told him, 'an' it ain't middle-aged neither.'

The episode had the poor fellow's mates doubled up laughing. Quickly, the blue-eyed man served them with their tennis balls and they left, no doubt to tease their unfortunate pal all the way home. Poor thing! How was he to know he'd made fun of the wrong woman? If it had been me, I'd have curled into a corner. 'Well!' Sonya demanded. 'Where can I try these on? I ain't buyin' 'em till I see what they looks like!'

In the end, she was allowed to creep behind the sock display. That was a mistake, because when she bent over to pull up the legs the whole lot came crashing down, and her with it. 'Some soddin' shop this is!' she told the blue-eyed man, whose vein looked fit to pop. 'Lock that bloody door, Jessica, afore anybody else comes in.'

When, wringing his hands together and running up and down, the blue-eyed man protested, 'Oh, madam! You can't do that!' she stripped her plum-coloured suit off and threw it at him.

''Ere . . . yer can put that back. It's bloody awful!' He then turned his face to the wall while she tried the orange flowery one on. 'What d'yer think, Jessica?' she asked, parading to and fro, and occasionally stopping to admire herself in the mirror. I gave her my honest opinion: that I would never have the nerve to wear it. 'That'll do fer me, gal!' she said, peeling it off and thumping the blue-eyed fellow in the back. 'Turn round, yer silly arse!' she told him scathingly. 'There's better men than you seen what's under *my* counter! I'll tek it. Come on, gerra move on!' When she swung the poor chap round, to confront him with a bulging bare bosom, it was all he could do to catch his breath.

'Madam!' he spluttered. 'Please . . . make yourself decent at once!'

She let out a great earth-shattering roar of laughter. 'Mek mesel' decent? Yer must be jokin', darlin' . . . I wouldn't 'ave 'alf as much fun!' She refused to budge until he'd given her a ten per cent discount. When we finally departed (I with a black suit with white piping) the blue-eyed man was in a dreadful state. Rivers of sweat were running down his face and staining his collar, and he couldn't keep a limb still. 'One session wi' me, an' 'ed be a new man!' Sonya declared. When I reminded her that only last night she had sworn her sole allegiance to Kelly, she giggled and slapped me heartily on the back. 'What the eye don't see, the 'eart don't grieve over!' she said. (Will she ever change?)

As we drew level with my house, Sonya pointed across the road. 'Look at that!' she said. 'Looks like Barny's ex-wife's got a foot back in the door.' It certainly seemed that way, because there he was, one hand under the brunette's elbow as she got out of the car, the other clutched round the handle of a rather cumbersome suit-case. 'Shame!' muttered Sonya. 'I were sure 'e 'ad 'is roving eye set on you!' I wasn't sure, but I had hoped it would all come right between us. 'Never mind, gal,' she said, 'a feller as'd try an' put yer outta business ain't worth botherin' about.' I couldn't really convince myself of that – after all, hadn't I done the very same thing to him when I first came to Casey's Court?

It had been a long day, and when I suggested we leave the jogging till tomorrow evening, instead of the morning, Sonya needed no persuading. 'I'm knackered!' she said, in her usual endearing manner. 'I think I'll go an' put me legs up.' Then, as she went away down the street, she gave a raucous laugh and called out, 'That's if I can find some bugger ter keep me company!' When, at that point, Mad Aggie appeared, Sonya shouted, 'Christ almighty, will yer look at that. It's enough ter put yer off yer bloody tea!' Then she disappeared inside and slammed the door.

'Where's Ethelbert?' I asked Maggie, seeing there were only she and the children in the parlour.

'They're going old-tyme dancing!' piped up Wilhelmina.

When I told her it was rude to interrupt, Tom said, 'Well, they are!'

And so they were. 'Ethelbert's coming for me at eight o'clock,' Maggie explained, adding that they would get

160

changed when they got there, as Ethelbert thought it was a good idea to take their best togs in a suitcase.

I thought it was a silly idea, and I told her so. 'Your best things will be all creased,' I warned her.

But she was adamant. 'We're going on the bus,' she said, 'and I'm not having everybody laughing at us dolled up like Fred Astaire and Ginger Rogers.' I was delighted that the old folks had found an outside interest, but, I had to admit, I was somewhat surprised by this sudden passion for old-tyme dancing. 'Not at all!' objected Maggie. 'I was quite a turn in my day . . . and it seems that my Ethelbert won prizes!'

At eight fifteen, off they went, all starry-eyed and obviously head over heels in love. They looked a lovely couple, Ethelbert with his black furry thing sticking out from beneath both sides of his flat cap and Maggie with her best blue two-piece on. She had her arm linked in his. He carried the suitcase, and she took charge of the cheese and pickle sandwiches, so lovingly prepared 'for during the interval', she explained. The sight of them, arm in arm, tripping down the street and gazing into each other's eyes, brought a lump to my throat. 'Don't wait up,' called Maggie, 'we won't be home for some time.'

As they passed Sonya at her door, she shouted, 'You watch 'im in that foxtrot . . . the bugger's craftier than any fox. An' don't let 'im fotch yer 'ome by way o' Tinkers Bridge – that's where 'e got Florrie Andover in trouble!' They weren't listening, though. They were too lost in each other.

It's now half past one in the morning and there's still no sign of them. I'm worried stiff. I rang Sonya up ten minutes ago; she was none too pleased. 'Fancy ringing me this time of a mornin'!' she said in a sleepy voice. 'I coulda been up to anythin'!'

161

'Oh, I am sorry,' I whispered. 'Have you got . . . company?'

''Ave I 'ell as like,' she retorted, 'but I were 'avin' a lovely dream.' Before she could launch into the lurid details, I expressed my concern that Maggie and Ethelbert still weren't back. 'Stop worryin', yer silly arse!' she chortled. 'I expect 'e's tekken 'er up Tinkers Bridge fer a bit of 'ow's yer father! They'll turn up, you'll see, when the 'edge'ogs start their wanderin'. Them bristles can give a body a nasty shock . . . an' I should know!'

'Oh, Sonya . . . are you sure? You're sure they have gone up Tinkers Bridge?'

'Course I am! Let the poor ol' sods 'ave their night on the town. Get back ter sleep, go on!'

I waited till two A.M. There's still no sign of Maggie. But perhaps Sonya's right. They are both adults, after all. And I can't keep my eyes open much longer. I'm tempted to go up Tinkers Bridge, but I don't think Maggie would thank me for it, somehow.

Wednesday, October 14th

It's been one thing after another today. Maggie was still missing when I woke up at six A.M. According to Sonya when I rang, Ethelbert hadn't come home either. She came straight round. 'It ain't like the ol' bugger,' she said. 'There's some'at wrong about this little lot.' So she took Wilhelmina to school while I put the closed sign up in the salon and called the authorities.

It was my favourite helmet who answered. 'This is getting to be a habit,' he said. I had a vivid image of him licking his pencil, ready to scribble in his note-pad. 'You never fail to amaze me, Mrs Jolly,' he went on in scathing tones. 'First you're drunk as a lord when the councillor calls on you. Then your daughter runs away . . . you get caught up in a street brawl . . . probably started it, I shouldn't be surprised. And now you've been careless enough to lose your ma-in-law. I shouldn't wonder if she's run away as well.' I never knew I had such a criminal record.

The conversation was very one-sided, with him indicating that I must be a bad lot and me protesting that I wasn't as black as he painted me. The upshot of it all was that he could do nothing until this evening. 'A person is not missing until they've been gone for twenty-four hours,' he said. However, he did sympathize. 'You keep me in touch,' he said, 'and if they turn up, let me know.'

I was frantic! By nine thirty there was still no sign of her. News of Maggie and Ethelbert's disappearance had spread like wildfire round Casey's Court. There must have been a hundred well-wishers knocking on the front door in a never-ending stream. They really are the kindest, most wonderful folk. All concerned, all ready with some comforting explanation or other. The woman from the tripe shop told me not to worry too much. 'That Ethelbert Pitts allus 'as been a randy little divil!' she said. 'I expect, if the truth be told, 'e 'ad 'is wicked way wi' your Maggie, an' they're both sleepin' it off in some field or other.'

Mrs Flannagan folded her huge fat arms across her mountainous breasts and told me, 'I've seen them two these last weeks, gazing into each other's eyes an' 'olding 'ands. I'm not agin it. Oh, no . . . don't think that. But if yer ask me, it's impossible ter see where yer going if yer busy scennin' at somebody else. I expect they've fell down a gurt 'ole. That's where they'll find Maggie an' Ethelbert Pitts! Down some bloody gurt 'ole . . . gazing into each other's eyes!'

Bertha Twistle waited till she'd gone, then said, 'Tek no notice o' that one, lass! She's only jealous. Fell down 'ole indeed! What nonsense! Naw . . . they've just been an' caught the wrong bus, that's all. They've probably been wanderin' atop the moors all night. They'll be 'ome in a while, you'll see!'

Fred Twistle said Ethelbert should have had more sense, having been in the army and all that. 'The silly sod's forgotten 'is basic trainin',' he said with some disgust. 'If yer not sure which way ter go yer should allus turn left. Keep turnin' left.' Immediately, there erupted a raging argument, one fellow pointing out that he couldn't remember ever being given such an instruction. And little Larkin quietly explained that if Maggie and Ethelbert had turned left from the Palais they'd end up at the bottom of the Cut. When the lady from the corner shop shouted her down, she burst into tears and fled indoors, leaving behind a gale force wind that dispersed the crowd in seconds. All but Fred Twistle, who stood his ground magnificently.

'That bloody Ethelbert's absent without leave!' he declared, waving his fist in the air. 'In my day that woulda meant a week in the glass'ouse!' He would have said more, but Bertha got him by the ear and dragged him away.

'Go an' talk ter yer pigeons!' she told him. ''Appen *they*'ll be interested in yer war-efforts.'

Sonya had the inspiration of organizing a search-party. In no time at all, all the young mums (and those amongst the elderly who could move a pace) were duly recruited. Sonya displayed extraordinary organizational skills, splitting the party into groups of four and sending them off in different directions. 'You an' me, gal,' she said, when all had departed, 'we'll cover the back alleys leadin' down ter the market square.' So off we went with the young ones in tow, and Lucky bounding away up front.

We didn't find Maggie and Ethelbert. But we found a flasher! A real live flasher, prancing stark naked in and out of the empty market stalls. 'Lord love us!' gasped Sonya. ''Ave yer ever seen owt like it?' No, I had to admit, I never had. How he had the strength to swing himself and that lot up into the roof structure, I do not know. Lucky yapped himself into a frenzy, and Tom burst into fits of tears. He was almost hysterical.

'Stop that at once!' I shouted, shaking him by the shoulders. 'What on earth's the matter with you?' He seemed to be in the grip of abject terror. When he'd calmed down enough to talk, I felt more sympathetic towards him. After all, he did have a point . . . I don't think I'd want a thingie like that either. And he was quite right – he wouldn't be able to get his little wellies on.

Sonya talked the fellow down. 'Don't worry about me,' she said, gripping him by the arm and propelling him away 'I'll be back later . . . I'll just make sure this bloke gets what's coming to 'im!' (She will, too. That'll teach him.)

When I got back home, there was a tall thin man with a moustache waiting at the door for me. 'Can I have a word, Mrs Jolly?' he asked politely. My first thought was for Maggie, but he assured me that his visit had nothing to do with any other member of the family. I ushered the little watchers into the scullery and sat them down with a cream-cake, while the visitor waited in the parlour. On my return, he explained that he was from the south, an official given the task of locating the woman who absconded from the asylum near where I used to live. I vaguely recalled the incident, related to me by Tiffany, but I assured the man that I knew nothing of the business.

'Are you quite certain you had no strangers at your door on the day you left the area?' he asked, explaining that everyone who had left the vicinity in that week was being traced; it wasn't just me in particular.

'No,' I told him, 'I saw no strangers at all. In fact, the only visitor I had just before leaving was my mother-in-law.'

He was satisfied, and apologized for disturbing me. Before I closed the door behind him, though, he turned and said, 'It's just as well that she didn't find her way to your house. The woman appears quite harmless, but is extremely dangerous. She has a particularly nasty habit of digging great holes, with the intention of burying her victims in them. She is totally insane, I'm afraid. Good day, Mrs Jolly.'

I was half way down the passage when the penny dropped. Dropped with such a clang that it sent me reeling against the wall. There *had* been a stranger at my door. I *did* know a woman who dug great holes! It was Maggie! *Maggie* – whom I believed straight away was Vernon Jolly's estranged mother because of her knowledge of him, and because of the photos she carried. But what if Maggie wasn't Vernon Jolly's mother? What if she'd elicited the information from him while he was rolling drunk? And what about all those odd little quirks of hers – running about with a tin hat on and shouting 'Rally the troops! Rally the troops!'? Oh my God! Was Maggie the escaped lunatic? I felt the colour drain from my face, and a terrible feeling of loneliness washed over me as I looked up and begged, 'Please don't let it be Maggie . . . please!'

The ringing of the phone brought me back with a jolt. When I rushed to answer it, I was astonished to find that it was Maggie. 'I'm sorry, darling,' she said, giggling at something that was going on in the background, 'I'm a bit tipsy . . . and I'm gloriously happy . . .'

'Where are you?' I shouted into the phone. My only instinct was to protect her. They mustn't get Maggie back. She mustn't be locked up in an asylum. 'Don't come home yet,' I told her. 'Tell me where you are, and I'll come to you.' You could have knocked me down with a feather when Ethelbert came on the phone.

'We're married!' he said, giggling. 'Maggie an' me are man an' wife. We've eloped to Gretna Green . . . an' we're 'avin' a party!'

Then Maggie came back on the phone. 'We thought you and Sonya might try and talk us out of it . . . so we ran off. I'm Mrs Pitts now, and nobody can touch me.' Of a sudden, her voice changed and, more quietly, she said, 'We're making our way home in the morning, on the coach. We should be back about nine P.M. Jessica . . . I hope you're not going to be cross with me . . . but I've been keeping a terrible secret from you. I've confessed everything to my darling Ethelbert, and he says I have to come clean with you as well. He promises I won't be punished for it. And he says if we're to make a success of our marriage, I've to confide everything in you, and make a brand new start.'

Oh my God! So she *is* the woman they're searching for. 'Maggie,' I said, 'listen to me carefully. Don't tell anybody else about your secret . . . nobody, do you understand?'

'Oh, I won't! I'm that ashamed, Jessica. I won't dare tell anybody but you and my Ethelbert. I've kept it secret all this time . . . oh, Jessica, they won't lock me away again, will they?' I told her to stop worrying – nobody was going to lock her away while I was around. 'I'll tell you everything when I get home,' she promised. 'Ethelbert says he'll be there to give me moral strength. Oh, I hope you don't think too badly of me when I tell you the awful things I've done!' she whispered – and then someone began playing a piano and a voice burst into song. I heard Ethelbert's voice calling 'See yer tomorrer!' and then the phone went dead.

'She's what!' Sonya sat bolt upright in the chair, her brown eyes popping out like king marbles.

'Ssh, Sonya,' I warned, 'I don't want the children wakened.' She had been shocked rigid when I told her about Maggie, and that there had been a man here from the authorities searching for her. 'Oh, Sonya, I can't let them take her away. She might be a bit eccentric at times . . . but she's not insane. I know she isn't.'

Sonya disagreed. '*I* think she's right off 'er bloody trolley,' she said, 'I allus 'ave. But she's my mam-in-law as well now. An' just let anybody try an' touch 'er, that's all. What! The buggers won't know what's 'it 'em!' (They don't come any more loyal than Sonya Pitts.)

Tomorrow night can't come fast enough for me. I'll have to dye Maggie's hair and keep her disguised. 'Till the heat's off, y'mean?' asked Sonya, obviously finding it all an adventure.

'We're not in Chicago,' I said, 'Maggie and Ethelbert are not Bonnie and Clyde.' I reckon Sonya's seen too many Humphrey Bogart films.

Thursday, October 15th

The salon was buzzing all day – they were even queuing out of the door. Everyone was thrilled and excited at the news of Maggie and Ethelbert's being wed. 'We'll give 'em a right party,' they all agreed. 'Send 'em on the road to ruin with a big bang!' Up went the laughter when somebody pointed out that they'd already had the big bang – all that was left was to keep the balloon afloat.

There was gossip, also, concerning Barny Singleton. And, if I hadn't been so worried about Maggie, I might have felt a tingle or two on hearing that his ex-wife had only been staying at his place because she'd sold her own house. She'd married this Aussie, who had gone back to Australia to get things ready for her and her son. The lad was going to spend nine months there and three with Barny from now on, and everybody was very pleased with the arrangement, Barny Singleton conceding that a young boy needed his mam and if the boy was happy, then so was he.

Wilhelmina came home from school wearing a prefect's badge. 'Where did you get that from?' I demanded, having visions of a slight and terrified child being punched in a corner and having her badge pinched.

'It's mine,' she argued. 'I earned it!'

'Hm! We'll see about that, young madam,' I said, and got straight on the phone to Mrs Hepher.

'It is hers,' she assured me. 'Your daughter has progressed immensely. Don't ask me what brought about the change in her . . . she's like a new girl.'

In a somewhat sheepish and embarrassed fashion I asked Wilhelmina's forgiveness and, cuddling her tight, promised I'd never mistrust her again. 'I'm very proud of you,' I told her, 'proud to call you my daughter.' (We both cried.)

'Silly cow!' said Sonya. 'Ye'll mek the kid soft!' (So what!)

Just after I'd washed up the tea things there came the sound of uproar from out in the street and, as I made my way up the passage to the front door, Sonya came bursting in. 'We're being invaded!' she shouted, waving two bits of paper in the air. 'The buggers want us out!' She thrust one of the papers under my nose. ''Ere . . . read that!' It was an official notification, addressed to all residents of Casey's Court, informing them of the Council's decision to 'demolish the area in favour of a redevelopment programme'. It also said that the decision was final, and delegates would be entering Casey's Court at 9 A.M. on Friday, October 16th to 'conduct an open meeting, when certain rehousing schemes would be put forward for discussion'.

'They've done it!' Sonya was in a fury. 'The buggers 'ave come down agin us!' In a minute, she had me by the arm and was dragging me into the street where every man, woman and child was congregating, all clutching the notifications, and all ready to take on the world.

'We'll fight ter the death afore we'll be shifted!' shouted one.

'Barricades! Put up the barricades!' shouted another. Everybody cheered and ran inside their houses to fetch all manner of things – chairs, tables, sideboards, and even a full-sized double bed. 'Seal off both ends o' Casey's Court!' went out the order, and in a matter of minutes it was done. Sonya and I rushed into the salon to carry out the two barber's chairs, which we piled up against the other paraphernalia. 'Yer a right little trooper, gal!' she said, giving me a bear-hug.

Everywhere was a hive of activity. People rushing and tearing about in all directions, sentries being posted all along the surrounding back alleys, where they stood facing the great cranes and bulldozers with brave faces and stout hearts. A deep voice from the top end began singing 'Land of Hope and Glory', and after the first shocked hush every voice was uplifted to join in . . . and it seemed as if the whole nation was there as the song

170

swelled to soar above the chimney-tops. I was so proud, I cried.

'Yer soft-arse!' laughed Sonya – but I noticed there were tears in her eyes too. 'Get ter yer station,' she said, 'an' keep the kids alongside yer!' They were loving every minute.

At quarter to ten, Maggie and Ethelbert appeared at the barricade. 'Christ almighty!' gasped Ethelbert, thinking all the fuss was for him and Maggie. 'We never expected a welcome like this!'

''Tain't fer you, yer great twaddle!' shouted Sonya. 'It's ter keep the Council an' its bulldozers out! Get yer arse over 'ere an' do yer stuff!'

He panicked, running up and down like a headless chicken and shouting, 'Me gun . . . where's me bloody gun?' Maggie was calling for her tin hat.

'You're a right bloody pair in any emergency, ain't yer?' snorted Fred Twistle with some disgust, as he helped Big Jack to drag the two of them over the barricades.

In no time at all they were composed, equipped, and in their places. 'We'll have to talk later,' Maggie said, placing a kiss on my cheek, and giving the children a hug. 'First things first, eh?' And with that we all settled down for the night.

Friday, October 16th

I'll never forget this day, not as long as I live!

At ten o'clock this morning, Casey's Court looked like a battle-field. On one side the residents, on the other the milkman, the postman (neither could get through), the entire deputation from the Council, the newspaper reporters and a representation of local bobbies (including my favourite helmet).

There were threats and shouts, cajoling and persuading, but nobody intended to give way. 'We'll talk only when you promise to give Casey's Court a second chance!' shouted a burly fellow from the front.

'That's right!' yelled another. 'Rebuild! Not demolish!' And everyone gave support by raising their voices to cheer.

The siege went on for another hour before the MP arrived. All he could do was to promise to 'take up the case on your behalf'. It was not enough.

While furtive talks went on, Granny Grabber had a field day and Mad Aggie kept us all entertained.

Suddenly Barny Singleton appeared on the enemy side. 'What's going on?' he was heard to ask (having been away overseeing the departure to Australia). When advised of the situation, and cautioned not to involve himself by my favourite helmet, everyone held their breath to see what his reaction would be. There wasn't a sound to be heard.

For a split second, his dark handsome eyes settled on me, sending my nerve ends into a tingling frenzy and making me blush fierce red. In a minute, he vaulted over the barricade, to a rousing cheer and hearty pats on the back. 'This is my territory,' he called back to the helmet, 'and Casey's Court folk are my folk!' which raised another roar of approval. Then he was lost in the surge.

Of a sudden, a cry went up from the vicinity of my salon. One of the burlier women posted at the rear burst into the street, holding a squirming bald fellow by the scruff of the neck. 'It's old Jake!' she said, ''im as drives that big caterpillar thing. Tried to sneak through. What'll I do with him?'

Somebody suggested, 'Tie him up in Jessica's parlour, and give him some'at to read!' and she disappeared back inside with him.

'I hope she doesn't give him my Legoland to play with,' moaned Tom.

'I don't want him playing with my Jackie doll, either!' stated madam, going a delicate shade of pink when a gangly boy with a shock of red hair and spots sidled up to her.

'Hello, Wilhelmina,' he said in an awkward voice. 'Can I stay with you?'

''Course you can, Darlow,' she told him, making room on the armchair. Well I never! A prefect called Darlow, eh? Looks as if the love-bug's bitten again.

At midday, the Council had had enough. They retired to chambers to review the situation. Three hours later they were back with a reprieve. Casey's Court had won – for the time being, at least. There was to be another meeting in the New Year, when everybody would be invited to express their views. Barny Singleton kissed me full on the mouth to celebrate. And he's taking me to the pictures on Saturday.

'Let's 'ave a street-party!' Sonya suggested, and in no time at all there was food and music, and everybody was having a whale of a time.

'Bloody marvellous, ain't it?' laughed the woman from the tripe shop. 'I ain't enjoyed mesel' so much since VE Day!'

Before all the lights went out, I knew who the knicker-pincher was. It was my own darling Maggie! That was her secret – and the fact that she'd spent six months inside one of Her Majesty's establishments for the very same. 'Oh, Maggie!' I said, laughing and crying at the same time. 'I love you!'

173

'I love you too!' she laughed. And to prove it she gave me a whole chestful of delicate frilly knickers. 'My Ethelbert prefers me in bloomers anyway,' she said. They weren't my style either, but Sonya took them back to her place.

'Some o' my fellers'll give their right arm ter be seen in these,' she roared.

Later when she'd had one over the eight, or, to put it in her own words, was 'pissed as a newt', she got all remorseful and apologetic. 'I'm cheap an' vulgar, ain't I, gal?' she asked, with a sorry look in her eye.

''Course not,' I told her.

'Oh, yes I am! But I can't change, gal,' she added, with a forlorn look, 'an' it's no use me tryin'.'

'And thank the Lord for it!' I told her with a lump in my throat, as I grabbed her in a cuddle. 'Sonya Pitts, I wouldn't have you any other way!'

'Cross yer 'eart?' she said.

'Cross my heart,' I told her, and she knew I meant it.

'We're good pals, you an' me, ain't we, eh?' she said, with a broad grin and a shake of her strawberry blonde head.

'The best, Sonya luv,' I said in my best Sonya voice, 'the bloody best!' Whereupon she gawped at me, and we both burst out laughing.

Later we found the little bald caterpillar driver huddled up in a corner of the parlour, reading my diaries – and doubled up in fits of laughter. 'Yer ought ter get these published!' he said. 'They're right bloody comical!'

'Hey, why not?' rejoined Sonya. 'But first get Maggie Thatcher ter ban the buggers. What! Ye'd mek a bloody fortune!'

Well now, *there*'s a thought.

PS: I think old Pops likes the idea. The diary's just been snatched up and thrown into the air by some unseen hand. 'He likes it! He does!' shouted Sonya. 'Ol' Pops allus used ter throw 'is flat cap in the air like that when 'e won at dominoes!'